Creed grinned at her.

"Just so I can get this straight," he said, reaching into the bag and pulling out a jeweler's box, which he opened, "you're saying no?"

She stared at the box he'd opened for her to view. It contained a heart-shaped diamond, which he was pretty proud of picking out this morning.

"Creed," she said, sounding shocked and choked up. He snapped the box shut and put it back in the bag.

"Too bad," he said. "The jeweler promised me no woman could say no to this ring. He said a woman would have to have a heart of stone to refuse it. He said—"

"You're crazy," Aberdeen said. "I knew it when I first met you. I know you're crazy, and I know better than to throw myself to the wind like this, but I'm going to ride this ride, cowboy, and I swear, if you turn out to be a weirdo, I'll be really ticked at you."

Dear Reader,

Thank you for picking up this Harlequin Professional Bull Riders limited-edition copy of *One Wild Bull Rider* featuring Matt Triplett, exclusive bonus content and $20 in added value coupons.

I love writing about bull riders! They were the tough and fearless guys you wanted to date in high school. Or at least I did. They were polite, and they worked hard. These regular guys usually grew up on farms and ranches, and they always had a strong connection to home and family. Riding bulls was a rite of passage—a challenge. When a man has guts and commitment, that's very attractive. And as far as I was concerned, bull riders were the guys to take home to mother—and my mother was picky as hell!

If you're as intrigued as I am by the thrilling sport of bull riding, be sure to visit the Professional Bull Riders, Inc. website at pbr.com. Don't forget to check out my next three limited-edition releases: *A Family for the Bull Rider*, *Heart of a Bull Rider*, and *The Bull Rider's Twins*, all available in stores now!

You can find more of my titles on my website at tinaleonard.com. I love interacting with readers! Please contact me at facebook.com/authortinaleonard, pinterest.com/tinaleonard1 and on Twitter, @Tina_Leonard.

Best wishes and happy reading!

Tina Leonard

ONE WILD BULL RIDER

USA TODAY BESTSELLING AUTHOR
TINA LEONARD

ISBN-13: 978-0-373-82666-7

One Wild Bull Rider

Copyright © 2011 by Tina Leonard

First published as The Cowboy's Bonus Baby
by Harlequin Books in 2011.

This edition published 2015.

Recycling programs
for this product may
not exist in your area.

HARLEQUIN®
™ www.Harlequin.com

Printed in U.S.A.

Tina Leonard is a *USA TODAY* bestselling and award-winning author of more than fifty projects, including several popular miniseries for the Harlequin American Romance line. Known for bad-boy heroes and smart, adventurous heroines, her books have made the *USA TODAY*, Waldenbooks, Ingram and Nielsen BookScan bestseller lists. Born on a military base, Tina lived in many states before eventually marrying the boy who did her crayon printing for her in the first grade. You can visit her at tinaleonard.com and follow her on Facebook, Pinterest and Twitter.

Books by Tina Leonard

Harlequin American Romance

Bridesmaids Creek

The Rebel Cowboy's Quadruplets
The SEAL's Holiday Babies
The Twins' Rodeo Rider
The Cowboy SEAL's Triplets

Callahan Cowboys

A Callahan Wedding
The Renegade Cowboy Returns
The Cowboy Soldier's Sons
Christmas in Texas
"Christmas Baby Blessings"
A Callahan Outlaw's Twins
His Callahan Bride's Baby
Branded by a Callahan
Callahan Cowboy Triplets
A Callahan Christmas Miracle
Her Callahan Family Man
Sweet Callahan Homecoming

Visit the Author Profile page
at Harlequin.com for more titles.

Many thanks to Kathleen Scheibling for believing
in the Callahan Cowboys series from the start.
I have certainly enjoyed the past five years under your
guidance. There are so many people at Harlequin who
make my books ready for publication, most of whom
I will never have the chance to thank
in person, and they have my heartfelt gratitude.
Also many thanks to my children and my husband,
who are enthusiastic and supportive. And most of all,
much appreciation to my generous readers,
who are the reason for my success.

Chapter One

"Creed is my wild child. He wants everything he can't have."

—Molly Callahan, with fondness,
about her busy toddler

Creed Callahan was running scared. Running wasn't his usual way of doing things, but Aunt Fiona's plot to get him and his five brothers married had him spooked. Marriage was a serious business, not to be undertaken lightly, especially by a commitment-phobe. Aunt Fiona had just scored a direct hit with Creed's brother Pete, who'd married Jackie Samuels and had triplets right off the baby-daddy bat. Creed was potently aware his days as a happy, freewheeling bachelor might come to an end if he didn't get the hell away from Rancho Diablo.

So he'd fled like a shy girl at her first dance. Creed didn't relish being called chicken, but Aunt Fiona was a force to be reckoned with. Creed stared into his sixth beer, which the bartender in Lance, Wyoming, a generous man who could see that Creed's soul was in torment, had courteously poured.

Anyone in Diablo, New Mexico, would attest to the powers of Aunt Fiona. Especially when she had a goal—

then no one was safe. His small, spare aunt had raised him and his five brothers upon the deaths of their parents without so much as a break in her stride. She and her butler, Burke, had flown in from Ireland one day, clucked over and coddled the five confused boys (young Sam had not yet been part of the family, an occurrence which still perplexed the brothers), and gave them an upbringing which was loving, firm and heaped with enthusiastic advice.

Creed barely remembered their parents, Jeremiah and Molly. He was the lucky one in the family, in his opinion, because he had a twin, Rafe. It had helped to have a mirror image at his back over the years. Creed was prone to mischief, Rafe was more of a thinker. Once, when the boys had wondered where babies came from—upon Sam's surprising arrival after Fiona had come to be their guardian—Creed had uprooted all of Fiona's precious garden looking for "baby" seeds. Rafe had told Aunt Fiona that he'd seen bunnies in her garden, which was true, but bunnies weren't the reason Aunt Fiona's kitchen crop had to be restarted.

Creed certainly knew where babies came from now. Watching Pete and Jackie go from a casual romance once a week to parents of triplets had underscored for him the amazing fertility of the Callahan men. They were like stallions—gifted with the goods.

With Fiona prodding about his unmarried state, Creed had hit the road. He did not want his own virility tested. He didn't want a wife or children. Pete was solidly positioned to win Rancho Diablo, for that was the deal Fiona had struck: whoever of the six brothers married and produced the most heirs inherited all five thousand acres.

But he and his brothers had worked an agreement

out unbeknownst to their wily aunt: Only one of them would be the sacrifice (which had turned out to be the lucky—or unlucky, depending upon how one viewed it—brother Pete), and he would divide the ranch between the six of them. It was a fair-and-square way to keep any animosity from arising between them for the high-value prize of hearth and home. Competition wasn't a good thing among brothers, they'd agreed, though they competed against each other all the time, naturally. But this was different.

This competition wasn't bull riding, or lassoing, or tree climbing. This was a race to the altar, and they vowed that Fiona's planning wouldn't entrap them.

"And I'm safe," Creed muttered into his beer.

"Did you say something?" a chocolate-haired beauty said to him, and Creed realized that the old saying was true: Women started looking better with every beer. Creed blinked. The male bartender who'd been listening to his woes with a sympathetic ear had morphed into a sexy female, which meant Creed wasn't as safe as he thought he was. He was, in fact, six sheets to the wind and blowing south. "Six beers is not that big a deal," he told the woman who was looking at him with some approbation. "Where's Johnny?"

"Johnny?" She raised elfin brows at him and ran a hand through springy chin-length curls. "My name is Aberdeen."

He wasn't *that* drunk. In fact, he wasn't drunk at all. He knew the difference between moobs and boobs, and while Johnny had been the soul of generosity, he'd had girth appropriate for bouncing troublemakers out of his bar. This delightful lady eyeing him had a figure, pert and enticing, and Creed's chauvinistic brain was regis-

tering very little else except she looked like something a
man who'd had six beers (okay, maybe twelve, but they
were small ones so he'd halved his count), might want
to drag into the sack. She had bow-shaped lips and dark
blue eyes, but, most of all, she smelled like something
other than beer and salami and pretzels. *Spring flowers,*
he thought with a sigh. Yes, the smells of spring, after a
long cold winter in Diablo. "You're beautiful," he heard
someone tell her, and glanced around for the dope that
would say something so unmanly.

"Thank you," she said to Creed.

"Oh, I didn't—" He stopped. *He* was the dope. *I sound
like Pete. I need to leave now.* The beer had loosened
his tongue and thrown his cool to the wind. "I'd best be
going, Amber Jean." He slid off the barstool, thinking
how sad it was that he'd never see Johnny/Amber Jean
again, and how wonderfully fresh and romantic springtime smelled in Wyoming.

"OH, NOW, THAT'S a shame," Johnny Donovan said,
looking down at the sleeping cowboy on his bar floor.
"Clearly this is a man who doesn't know much about
brew."

Aberdeen gave her brother a disparaging glance.
"You're the one who gave him too much."

"I swear I did not. The man wanted to talk more than
drink, truthfully." Johnny gave Aberdeen his most in-
nocent gaze. "He went on and on and on, Aberdeen,
and so I could tell he wasn't really looking for the hops
but for a good listener. On his fifth beer, I began giving
him near-beer, as God is my witness, Aberdeen. You
know I disapprove of sloppiness. And it's against the
law to let someone drink and drive." He squinted out-

side, searching the darkness. It was three o'clock in the morning. "Mind you, I have no idea what he's driving, but he won't be driving a vehicle from my bar in this sloppy condition."

Her brother ran a conscientious establishment. "I'm sorry," Aberdeen said, knowing Johnny treated his patrons like family. Even strangers were given Johnny's big smile, and if anyone so much as mentioned they needed help, Johnny would give them the shirt off his back and the socks off his feet. Aberdeen looked at the cowboy sprawled on the floor, his face turned to the ceiling as he snored with luxuriant abandon. He was sinfully gorgeous: a pile, at the moment, of amazing masculinity. Lean and tall, with long dark hair, a chiseled face, a hint of being once broken about the nose. She restrained the urge to brush an errant swath of midnight hair away from his closed eyes. "What do we do with him?"

Johnny shrugged. "Leave him on the floor to sleep. The man is tired, Aberdeen. Would you have us kick a heartbroken soul out when he just needs a bit of time to gather his wits?"

"Heartbroken?" Aberdeen frowned. The cowboy was too good-looking by half. Men like him demanded caution; she knew this from her congregation. Ladies loved the cowboys; they loved the character and the drive. They loved the romance, the idea of the real working man. And heaven only knew, a lot of those men loved the ladies in return. This one, with his soft voice, good manners and flashing blue eyes…Well, Aberdeen had no doubt that this cowboy had left his fair share of broken hearts trampled in the dirt. "If you sit him outside, he'll gather his wits fast enough."

"Ah, now, Aberdeen. I can't treat paying customers

that way, darling. You know that. He's causing no harm, is he?" Johnny looked at her with his widest smile and most apologetic expression, which should have looked silly on her bear of a brother, but which melted her heart every time.

"You're too soft, Johnny."

"And you're too hard, my girl. I often ask myself if all cowboy preachers are as tough on cowboys as you are. This is one of your flock, Aberdeen. He's only drunk on confusion and sadness." Johnny stared at Creed's long-forgotten beer mug. "I feel sorry for him."

Aberdeen sighed. "It's your bar. You do as you like. I'm going to my room."

Johnny went on sweeping up. "I'll keep an eye on him. You go on to bed. You have preaching to do in the morning."

"And I haven't finished writing my sermon. Good-night, Johnny." She cast a last glance at the slumbering, too-sexy man on the dark hardwood floor, and headed upstairs. She was glad to leave Johnny with the stranger. No man should look that good sleeping on the floor.

A ROAR FROM DOWNSTAIRS, guffaws and loud thumping woke Aberdeen from deep sleep. Jumping to her feet, she glanced at her bedside clock. Seven o'clock—past time for her to be getting ready for church. She grabbed her robe, and more roars sent her running down the stairs.

Her brother and the stranger sat playing cards on a barrel table in the empty bar. One of them was winning—that much was clear from the grins—and the other didn't mind that he was losing. There were mugs of milk and steaming coffee on a table beside them. Both men were so engrossed in their game that neither of them looked up as she stood there with her hands on her hips. She was of half a mind to march back upstairs and forget she'd ever seen her brother being led astray by the hunky stranger.

"Johnny," Aberdeen said, "did you know it's Sunday morning?"

"I do, darlin'," Johnny said, "but I can't leave him. He's got a fever." He gestured to his playing partner.

"A fever?" Aberdeen's eyes widened. "If he's sick, why isn't he in bed?"

"He won't go. I think he's delirious."

She came closer to inspect the cowboy. "What do you mean, he won't go?"

"He thinks he's home." Johnny grinned at her. "It's the craziest thing."

"It's a lie, Johnny. He's setting us up." She slapped her hand on the table in front of the cowboy. He looked up at her with wide, too-bright eyes. "Have you considered he's on drugs? Maybe that's why he passed out last night."

"Nah," Johnny said. "He's just a little crazy."

She pulled up a chair, eyeing the cowboy cautiously, as he eyed her right back. "Johnny, we don't need 'a little crazy' right now."

"I know you're worried, Aberdeen."

"Aberdeen," the cowboy said, trying out her name. "Not Amber Jean. Aberdeen."

She looked at Johnny. "Maybe he's slow."

Johnny shrugged. "Said he got a small concussion at his last stop. Got thrown from a bull and didn't ride again that night. He says he just had to come home."

She shook her head. "Sounds like it might be serious. He could have a fever. We can't try to nurse him, Johnny."

"We can take him to the hospital, I suppose." Johnny looked at the stranger. "Do you want to go to a hospital, friend?"

The cowboy shook his head. "I think I'll go to bed now."

Aberdeen wrinkled her nose as the cowboy went over to a long bench in the corner, laid himself out and promptly went to sleep. "You were giving milk to a man with fever?"

Johnny looked at her, his dark eyes curious. "Is that a bad thing? He asked for it."

She sighed. "We'll know soon enough." After a moment, she walked over and put her hand against his forehead. "He's burning up!"

"Well," Johnny said, "the bar's closed today. He can sleep on that bench if he likes, I guess. If he's not better tomorrow, I'll take him to a doctor, though he doesn't seem especially inclined to go."

Aberdeen stared at the sleeping cowboy's handsome face. *Trouble with a capital T.* "Did he tell you his name? Maybe he's got family around here who could come get him."

"No." Johnny put the cards away and tossed out the milk. "He babbles a lot about horses. Talks a great deal about spirit horses and other nonsense. Native American lore. Throws in an occasional Irish tale. Told a pretty funny joke, too. The man has a sense of humor, even if he is out of his mind."

"Great." Aberdeen had a funny feeling about the cowboy who had come to Johnny's Bar and Grill. "I'm going to see who he is," she said, reaching into his front pocket for his wallet.

A hand shot out, grabbing her wrist. Aberdeen gasped and tried to draw away, but the cowboy held on, staring up at her with those navy eyes. She couldn't look away.

"Stealing's wrong," he said.

She slapped his hand and he released her. "I know that, you ape. What's your name?"

He crossed his arms and gave her a roguish grin. "What's *your* name?"

"I already told you my name is Aberdeen." He'd said it not five minutes ago, so possibly he did have a concussion. With a fever, that could mean complications. "Johnny, this man is going to need a run to the—"

The cowboy watched her with unblinking eyes. Aberdeen decided to play it safe. "Johnny, could you pull the truck around? Our guest wants to go for a ride to see our good friend, Dr. Mayberry."

Johnny glanced at the man on the bench. "Does he now?"

"He does," Aberdeen said firmly.

Johnny nodded and left to get his truck. Aberdeen looked at the ill man, who watched her like a hawk. "Cowboy, I'm going to look at your license, and if you grab me again like you did a second ago, you'll wish you hadn't. I may be a minister, but when you live above a bar, you learn to take care of yourself. So either you give me your wallet, or I take it. Those are your choices."

He stared at her, unmoving.

She reached into his pocket and pulled out his wallet, keeping her gaze on him, trying to ignore the expanse of wide chest and other parts of him she definitely shouldn't notice. Flipping it open, she took out his driver's license. "Creed Callahan. New Mexico."

She put the license away, ignoring the fact that he had heaven-only-knew-how-many hundred-dollar bills stuffed into the calfskin wallet, and slid it back into his pocket.

He grabbed her, pulling her to him for a fast kiss. His lips molded to hers, and Aberdeen felt a spark—more than a spark, *real* heat—and then he released her.

She glared at him. He shrugged. "I figured you'd get around to slapping me eventually. Might as well pay hell is what I always say."

"Is that what you always say? With every woman you force to kiss you?" Aberdeen asked, rattled, and even more irritated that she hadn't been kissed like that in years. "You said stealing was wrong."

"It is. I didn't say I didn't do it." He grinned, highly pleased with himself, and if he hadn't already rung his bell, she would have slapped him into the next county.

Then again, it was hard to stay mad when he was that cheerful about being bad. Aberdeen put her hands on her hips so he couldn't grab her again. "All right, Mr. Callahan, do you remember why you're in Wyoming?"

"To ride the bulls. I ride, ma'am. There's an event in town."

Johnny was back. "Truck's out front."

"Johnny," Aberdeen said, "this is Creed Callahan. Mr. Callahan is very happy you're going to take him for a ride. Aren't you, Mr. Callahan?"

"Callahan?" Johnny repeated. "One of the six Callahans from New Mexico?"

"Have you heard of him?"

"Sure." Johnny shrugged. "All of them ride bulls, and

not too shabbily. The older brother didn't ride much, but he did a lot of rodeo doctoring after he got out of medical school. Some of them have been highly ranked. You don't go to watch bull riding without knowing about the Callahans." He looked at Creed with sympathy. "What are you doing here, friend?"

Creed sighed. "I think I'm getting away from something, but I can't remember what."

"A woman?" Johnny asked, and Aberdeen waited to hear the answer with sudden curiosity.

"A woman," Creed mused. "That sounds very likely. Women are trouble, you know. They want to have—" He lowered his voice conspiratorially in an attempt to keep Aberdeen from hearing. "They want to have b-a-b-i-e-s."

Aberdeen rolled her eyes. "Definitely out of his mind. Take him away, Johnny."

Her brother laughed. "He may be right, you know."

"I don't care," Aberdeen said, gathering her self-control. He might have stolen a kiss, but the conceited louse was never getting another one from her. "He's crazy."

"That's what they say," Creed said, perking up, obviously recognizing something he'd heard about himself before.

Aberdeen washed her hands of Mr. Loco. "Goodbye, cowboy," she said, "hope you get yourself together again some day. I'll be praying for you."

"And I'll be praying for you," Creed said courteously, before rolling off the bench onto the floor.

"That's it, old man," Johnny said, lifting Creed up and over his shoulder. "Off we go, then. Aberdeen, I may not make your service today, love."

"It's okay, Johnny." Aberdeen watched her brother

carry Creed to the truck and place him inside as carefully as a baby. The man said he was running, but no one ran from their family, did they? Not someone who had five brothers who'd often traveled together, rode together, competed against each other? And Johnny said one of the brothers was a doctor.

People needed family when they were hurting. He'd be better off with them instead of being in Wyoming among strangers.

Aberdeen went to her room to look up Callahans in New Mexico, thinking about her own desire for a family. A real one. Her sister, Diane, had tried to make a family, but it hadn't worked. Though she had three small adorable daughters, Diane wasn't cut out to be a mother. Then Aberdeen had married Shawn "Re-ride" Parker right out of high school. That hadn't lasted long, and there had been no children. And Johnny, a confirmed bachelor, said he had enough on his hands with his two sisters. They had their own definition of family, Aberdeen supposed, which worked for them. If a woman was looking to be have a baby, though, Creed Callahan probably ranked as perfect donor material—if a woman liked crazy, which she didn't. "I don't do crazy anymore," she reminded herself, dialing the listing she got from the operator.

The sooner crazy left town, the better for all of them.

Chapter Two

Creed was astonished to see his brother Judah when he awakened. He was even more surprised to realize he was in a hospital room. He glanced around, frowning at his snoozing brother—Judah looked uncomfortable and ragged in the hospital chair—and wondered why he was here. Creed tried to remember how he'd gotten to the hospital and couldn't. Except for a ferocious headache, he felt fine.

"Judah," he said, and his brother started awake.

"Hey!" Judah grinned at him. "What the hell, man? You scared me to death."

"Why?" Creed combed his memory and found it lacking. "What's going on? Where am I?"

"We're in Lance, Wyoming. A bar owner brought you in."

"Was I in a fight?" Creed rubbed at his aching head, confused by his lost memory. He didn't remember drinking all that much, but if a bar owner had brought him in, maybe he'd gotten a little riled up. "If I was, I hope I won."

Judah smirked. "The fight you were in was apparently with a bull. And you lost. At least this round."

Creed perked up. "Which bull was it? I hope it was a bounty bull. At least a rank bull, right?"

His brother smiled. "Can I get you something? Are you hungry?"

Creed blinked. Judah didn't want to tell him which bull had thrown him, which wasn't good. Cowboys loved to brag, even on the bad rides. He told himself he was just a little out of practice, nothing more riding couldn't cure. "I feel like my head isn't part of my body."

"You've got a slight concussion. The doctor thinks you're going to be fine, but he's keeping you a few hours for observation."

"I've had concussions before and not gone to the hospital."

"This time you had a high fever. Could have been the concussion, could have been a bug. The doctors just want to keep an eye on you. They mapped your brain, by the way, and said you don't have too much rattling around inside your skull. The brain cavity is strangely lacking in material."

Creed grunted at Judah's ribbing. "Sorry you had to make the trip."

"No problem. I wasn't doing anything."

Creed grunted again at the lie. Callahans always had plenty to do around Rancho Diablo. Five thousand acres of prime land and several hundred head of livestock meant that they stayed plenty busy. They kept the ranch running through sheer hard work and commitment to the family business.

"Anyway, it's been a while since anyone's seen you. Didn't know where you were keeping yourself." Judah scrutinized him. "We really didn't understand why you left in the first place."

Now *that* Creed could dig out of his cranium. "I was next on Fiona's list, Judah. I could *feel* it." He shuddered. "You don't understand until you've had Fiona's eye trained on you. Once she's thinking about getting you to the altar, you're halfway there."

"She's thinking about all of us," Judah pointed out. "Remember, that's her plan."

"But it was supposed to be over when Pete got married. He was the sacrifice." Creed took a deep breath. "And then I realized Fiona was running through her catalog of eligible females for me. I could hear her mind whirring. I've known every woman Fiona could possibly think of all my life. And there's not a one of them I'd care to marry."

Judah nodded. "I feel the same way."

Creed brightened. "You do?"

"Sure. Occasionally I think about a certain gal, but then I think, no, she'd never have me. And then I get over it pretty fast." Judah grinned. "The sacrifice wasn't ever going to be me. I'm not good at commitment for the sake of just having a girl around. Heck, I was never even good at picking a girl to take to prom."

"That was an exercise in futility." Creed remembered his brother's agony. "I had to fix you up with some of my friends."

"And that was embarrassing because of you being a year older than me."

"I didn't exactly mind," Creed hedged. "And I didn't hear you complaining about going out with an older woman."

Judah shook his head. "My dates didn't complain because I'm a good kisser. When you're a year younger than the girls you take out, you learn to make it up to

them." He grinned. "You know, it's not that I don't like women, I just like *all* women."

"Amen, bro," Creed said happily, back on terra firma. "Women are a box of candy, you never know what you're going to get."

"All right, Forrest Gump. Go back to sleep." Judah smiled at the nurse who came in to take his brother's temperature. "I had no idea the ladies in Wyoming are so lovely," Judah said. "Why wasn't I living here all my life?"

Creed grinned at his brother's flirting. *Now* he remembered who he was. He was Creed Callahan, hotshot bull rider and serious serial lover of females. Wild at heart. It was good to be a Callahan. He was love-them-and-leave-them-happy, that's who he was.

And women adored him.

Creed never noticed the nurse taking his pulse and his temperature. Somewhere in his memory a vision of a brunette with expressive eyebrows nagged at him. A female who hadn't quite adored him. In fact, she might even have thought he was annoying.

It wasn't likely such a woman existed, but then again, he couldn't remember ever getting concussed by anything other than a rank bull, either. Creed closed his eyes, wishing his headache would go away, but there was greater pain inside him: His last several rides had been bombs. Not even close to eights. On par with unfortunate.

I need a break, and the only thing I manage to break is my head.

He'd just lie here and think about it a little while longer, and maybe the fog would lift. He heard Judah and the nurse giggling quietly about something, which didn't help. Judah could score any time he liked. The ladies loved all that haunted-existentialist crap that his younger brother exuded. *But I'm not existential. Rafe, he's an existential thinker. Me, I'm just wild. And that's all I'll ever be.*

He felt really tired just connecting those pieces of information. When he got out of here, he was going to remember that a fallen rider needed to get right back up on his reindeer.

Or something like that.

But then Creed thought about dark-blue annoyed eyes staring at him, and wondered if he was running out of good luck.

ABERDEEN SAT RELUCTANTLY at the cowboy's bedside, waiting for him to waken, and not really wanting him to. There was something about him that nagged at her, and it wasn't just that he'd kissed her. Cowboys were typically a good group, but she wasn't sure about this one, though she was trying to give him the benefit of the doubt. She worked to spread faith and good cheer amongst her beat-up flock, and beat-up they were on Sunday mornings. Her congregation consisted of maybe twenty-five people on a busy Sunday, often less. Banged-up gentlemen dragged in for an hour of prayer and sympathy and the potluck spaghetti lunch she and her friends served in the bar afterward. She preached in Johnny's big barn, which had a covered pavilion for indoor riding. The cowboys and cowgirls, wearing jeans and sleepy expressions of gratitude, gratefully headed to the risers.

This man was beat-up, all right, but he didn't seem like he cared to find spiritual recovery in any form. She pondered her transient congregation. Sunday mornings were her favorite part of the week, and she rarely ever missed giving a sermon, though if she did, Johnny was an excellent stand-in, as well as some of their friends. Neither of them had grown up thinking they wanted to be preachers, but missionarying had taken hold of Aberdeen in high school, growing stronger during college. She'd majored in theology, minored in business, and Johnny had done the opposite. The two of them were a good working team. Over the years, Johnny's Bar and Grill had become known as the place to hang out six days a week, crash when necessary, and hear words of worship on Sunday. Aberdeen knew many of the cowboys that pulled through Lance. She couldn't understand why she'd never heard of the Callahans, if they were the prolific, daring riders that Johnny claimed they were.

But she'd gotten busy in the past five years, so busy she barely paid attention to anything more than what the top bull riders were scoring, and sometimes not even that. Her knowledge had ebbed when she started helping Johnny at the bar and writing more of her sermons. She was twenty-nine, and at some point, she'd begun to focus more on her job and less on fun—although sometimes she missed fun. A lot.

Plus she had Diane to think about. Diane was in trouble, real trouble, and nothing she or Johnny did seemed to help her. Their older sister couldn't keep a job, couldn't keep a husband—she was on her third—and had three young children, had had one a year for the past three years. Now she was going through a bitter divorce from a man who'd walked out and was never coming back. It had always been hard for Aberdeen and Johnny to understand why Diane made the choices she did.

Recently, Diane had asked Aberdeen to adopt her

daughters, Ashley, Suzanne and Lincoln Rose. Diane said she could no longer handle the responsibility of being a parent. Aberdeen was seriously considering taking the girls in. If Diane didn't want to be a mother, then Aberdeen didn't want to see Child Protective Services picking up her nieces. She loved them, with all her heart.

Diane lived in Spring, Montana, and wanted to move to Paris to chase after a new boyfriend she'd met traveling through the state. Aberdeen lived in fear that their elderly parents would call and say that Diane had already skipped.

"Howdy," the cowboy said, and Aberdeen's gaze snapped up to meet his.

"Hi. Feeling better?" she asked, conscious once again of how those dark denim eyes unsettled her.

"I think so." He brightened after feeling his head. "Yes, I definitely am. Headache is gone." He gave her a confiding grin. "I dreamed about you."

Her mouth went dry. "Why?"

"I remembered your eyes. I didn't remember a lot else, but I did remember your eyes."

She'd remembered his, too, though she'd tried not to. "Good dream or a bad dream?"

He grinned. "Now, sugar, wouldn't you like to know?"

She pursed her lips, wishing she hadn't asked.

"Ah, now that's the expression I recall with clarity," Creed said. "Annoyance. Mainly because it's not what I usually see in a woman's eyes."

"No? What do you usually see?" Aberdeen *was* annoyed, and the second she fell into his trap, she was even more irritated. Mainly with herself.

"Lust, preacher lady. I see lust."

She leaned away from him. "Ladies do not lust."

He raised jet-black brows. "I swear they do."

"They desire," she told him. "They have longings."

He shook his head. "You've been meeting the wrong kind of fellows, sugar cake."

She got up and grabbed her purse. "It's good to see you on the mend, Mr. Callahan. Happy trails."

He laughed, a low, sensual sound that followed Aberdeen to the door. "Thank you, miss."

He hadn't placed an emphasis on *miss,* but it teed her off just the same. Made her feel naked. She wasn't an old-maid kind of miss; she was a conscientious abstainer from another marriage. *That's right, cowboy. I'm single and okay with it. Almost okay with it, anyway.*

As she rounded the corner, she plowed into a tall cowboy who looked a lot like the one she'd left in his hospital room.

"Whoa, little lady," he said, setting her back on her feet. "Where's the fire?"

She frowned. "You're not one of the Callahans, are you?"

"I am." He nodded, smiling at her. "You must be the nice lady who let us know Creed was down on his luck."

"Yes, I did. He's made a great recovery."

He tipped his hat, dark-blue eyes—just like Creed's— sparkling at her. "My name is Judah Callahan."

She reached out to shake his hand. "Aberdeen Donovan."

"We can't thank you enough, Miss Aberdeen."

He had kind eyes—unlike the flirt back in the hospital bed. "No thanks necessary. My brother Johnny would help anyone in trouble." She smiled at him. "I've got to run, but it was nice meeting you, Judah."

to the floor. "Not so fast, my friend," Creed said. "You haven't paid for your drink."

"Who are you?" The thief scrambled to his feet.

"Who are you?" Creed asked. "The bar's closed. Didn't you see the sign?"

"I—I wasn't doing anything wrong. I was just wetting my whistle."

"Do you do this often?" Creed asked. "Because I think the owners might object."

"They don't care. They give me free drinks all the time." He backed toward the window where he'd let himself in, realizing he wasn't going to get past Creed and his broom.

Creed put the handle out, tripping the man from behind. "Why do they give you free drinks, friend?"

"Because I was married to Aberdeen. And I'm going to marry her again. So I have a right to be here," he asserted, and Creed's heart went still in his chest.

"Are you telling the truth?"

"I never lie," the stranger said. "Anyway, I'm sorry I bothered you. I'll just be leaving the way I came in now."

Creed flipped on the lights, curious to see the man Aberdeen was going to marry. They stared at each other, sizing up the competition. "I'll be damned. I know you," Creed said, "you're that dime-store cowboy they call Re-ride."

"And you're a Callahan." Re-ride looked none too happy. "What are you doing in Aberdeen's bar?"

"Keeping it free of snakes." Creed felt the interview to be most unpleasant at this point. He almost wished he'd never heard the man break in. Marry Aberdeen? Surely she wouldn't marry this poor excuse for a cowboy.

Then again, she'd married him before, or at least that's what he claimed. It was something else Creed hadn't known about her. To be honest, Creed hadn't proven himself to be any more of a serious cowboy in Aberdeen's eyes after his rambling night on the plank bench. Aberdeen probably thought he was just as loose as Re-ride.

That didn't sit too well. "Go on," he told Re-ride. "Get out of my face. I'd beat you with this broom, but I've never roughed up a lady and I'm not going to start tonight. So *git*."

Re-ride looked like he was about to take exception to Creed's comment, then thought better of it and dove out the window. Creed locked it behind him—and this time, he turned on the security system. He couldn't risk more varmints crawling into the bar tonight—he was in too foul a mood to put up with nonsense. He put himself to bed in the guest room, feeling quite out of sorts about life in general.

Babies, beer burglars and a one-time bride—sometimes, life just handed a cowboy lemonade with no sugar in sight.

"I'VE LOOKED OVER these papers with Sam," Jonas said to Aunt Fiona, "and I think we're selling ourselves short. Maybe."

His aunt looked at him. "How?"

"We should fight it, for one thing. Not roll over for the state or Bode Jenkins. And I'm in a fighting mood. Now that I've sold my medical practice, I have more time to help you with things," Jonas said. "I should have been more available for you all along."

Fiona looked at her oldest nephew. "It shouldn't have

necessitated your attention. Darn Bode Jenkins's hide, anyway."

Jonas leaned against the kitchen counter, eyeing his small, spare aunt. She was like a protective bear overseeing her cubs, but actually, things should be the other way around. He and his brothers needed to be protecting her and Burke, now in their golden years. Fiona had tried to convince them that she was one foot from the grave, but he'd been keeping an eye on her, and he was pretty certain Fiona was working their heartstrings. She had never seemed healthier, other than an unusually low spirit for her, which he attributed to her concern about losing the ranch.

He had decided to lift those burdens from his diminutive, sweetly busybodying aunt. "You know that land I put an offer on?"

Fiona brightened. "Yes. East of here. How's that coming?"

"I've changed my mind," Jonas said, after a thoughtful pause. It took him a minute to get his head around the words; every day since he'd made the decision, he'd pondered the situation again and again. "I've withdrawn my offer."

Fiona's eyes widened. "For heaven's sakes, why?"

"Because we're not going anywhere," Jonas said. "That's how Creed feels, and I agree with him."

"Creed! He's had a concussion recently," Fiona said with a sniff. "He's not thinking straight. Then again, when does he?"

"I think he might be thinking straighter than all of us." Jonas reached over and patted her shoulder. "I'm going to need all my resources, both time and money, to fight this theft of our land. I don't regret giving up on Dark Diablo for a minute."

Fiona looked at him. "Dark Diablo? It sounds beautiful."

He thought again about the wide expanse of open land where he could run cattle and horses and have his own place. His own sign hanging over the drive, shouting to the world that this was Dark Diablo, his own spread. But Creed had said Rancho Diablo was their home, and that they should fight for it, and fight hard. They would have to be dragged off their land—instead of rolling over because things looked dark and done. "Otherwise," Creed had said, "we're just cowards. Runners. The family stays together," he'd said. "Sic Sam on them."

Jonas's jaw had dropped. Sam didn't get "sicced" on anyone. Sam liked to ignore the fact that he'd gone to law school, barely broke a sweat passing the bar, and then gone on to prestigious internships, working his way up to cases that garnered him credit for being a steely defender who never failed to make his opponents cry. He'd become famous for his big persona. But only his family had noticed that with every big win to his credit, he became unhappier.

Sam liked winning. Yet he didn't like defending corporate cases where he knew the little guy was getting strung. And after a particularly nasty case, Sam had packed it in. Come home to Rancho Diablo to recover from big-city life. Now he mostly acted as though he hadn't a care in the world.

Except for Rancho Diablo.

Jonas winced. They couldn't sic Sam on Bode, but they could fight. "I've been thinking, Aunt Fiona, and

I'm not so certain your marriage scheme doesn't have some merit."

She radiated delight. "Do you think so?"

He shrugged. "It wouldn't be as easy for the state to take a property where there are families. I'm not saying that they care about us, but it certainly makes it easier to win public sympathy when folks realize what happens to us here could happen to them."

"Yes, but Pete doesn't even live here with his family," she said, her shoulders sagging. "And the rest of you are short-timers."

He grinned. "Are you hosting a pity party, Aunt?"

She glared at him. "What if I am? It's my party, and I can cr—"

"When Creed gets back here in a few days, we'll throw that bachelor ball you wanted."

"Really?" Fiona clapped her hands.

"Sure. He needs to settle down."

She looked at him, suspicious. "Why him?"

"He wants to settle down more than anyone. Haven't you noticed? And his days of bull riding are over, though he'll never admit it. A woman would keep him off the road, and children would keep him busy."

"It's a great plan," Fiona said, "if you think it would work."

Better him than me. With Fiona busy with her usual plotting and planning, I'll try to figure out how to undo this problem with the ranch.

He was going to have to take a firm hand with his aunt and Burke. They weren't telling everything they knew. It was a riddle wrapped inside a mystery, but he agreed with Creed on one thing: It was better to fight than run.

AFTER A COUPLE more beers to help get him over the shock of Aberdeen's babies and the ex-husband who wanted her back, Creed decided maybe he'd be wiser to run than fight. It was three in the morning, but he couldn't sleep, and if he didn't quit thinking about her, he was going to end up having beer for breakfast. Creed sighed, not having any fun at all. Aberdeen tortured him, and she didn't even know it.

"I wouldn't be so bothered if it wasn't for Re-ride," he told a small pink stuffed bear he'd found underneath the coffee table—probably the smallest damsel's bear. He'd placed the bear on the coffee table after he'd discovered it. The bear had looked forlorn and lost without its tiny owner, so Creed had propped it on a stack of books, regarding it as he would a comforting friend. "You have to understand that the man is given to useless. Simply useless."

The bear made no reply but that was to be expected from stuffed pink bears, Creed told himself, and especially at this hour. And the bear was probably tired of hearing him debate his thoughts, because Creed was certainly tired of himself. Everything ran through his mind without resting, like a giant blender churning his conscience. "She's just so pretty," he told the bear, "I don't see what she sees in him. It's something she doesn't see in me." He considered that for a moment, and then said, "Which is really unfortunate, for me and for her. I am the better man, Bear, but then again, a woman's heart is unexplainable. I swear it is."

If his brothers were here, he could talk this over with them. They wouldn't be sympathetic, but they would clap him on the back, rib him mercilessly or perhaps offer him some advice—and at least he'd feel better. It

"Thank you, Aberdeen. Again, thanks for rescuing Bubba."

She shook her head and walked away. Bubba. There was nothing little-brother Bubba about Creed. He was all full-grown man and devil-may-care lifestyle. She'd be a fool to fall for a man like him. Fortunately, forewarned was forearmed.

Chapter Three

Judah strolled into Creed's room. By the sneaky smile on his brother's face, Creed deduced that his visit wasn't all about rousing the patient to better health. "What?" Creed had a funny feeling he knew what was coming.

"You've got all the luck," Judah said, throwing himself into a chair. "Finding a little angel like that to rescue you."

Judah grinned, but Creed let his scowl deepen. "She's not as much of an angel as she appears. Don't let her looks fool you."

His brother laughed. "Couldn't sweet-talk her, huh?"
Creed sniffed. "Didn't try."

"Sure you did." Judah crossed a leg over a knee and lounged indolently, enjoying having Creed at his mercy. "She didn't give you the time of day." He looked up at the ceiling, putting on a serious face. "You know, some ladies take their angel status very seriously."

"Meaning?" Creed arched a brow at his brother, half-curious as to where all this ribbing was going. Judah had no room to talk about success with women, as far as Creed was concerned. Only Pete was married—and only Pete had claimed a girlfriend, sort of, before Aunt Fiona had thrown down the marriage gauntlet. Creed figured the rest of the Callahan brothers were just about nowhere with serious relationships.

Including me.

"Just that once a woman like her rescues a man, she almost feels responsible for him. Like a child." Judah sighed. "Very difficult thing to get away from, when a woman sees a man in a mothering light."

Creed stared at his brother. "That's the biggest bunch of hogwash I've ever heard."

"Have you ever wondered exactly what hogwash is?" Judah looked thoughtful. "If I had a hog, I sure wouldn't wash it."

"Hogwash just means garbage," Creed said testily. "Your literal mood is not amusing."

"I was just making conversation, since you're not in a position to do much else."

"Sorry." Creed got back to the point he was most intrigued by. "Anyway, so you met Aberdeen?"

Judah nodded. "Yes. And thanked her for taking care of my older brother. Do you remember any of what happened to you?"

"I don't know. Some bug hit me, I guess." Creed was missing a couple of days out of his life. "I didn't make the cut in Lance, so I was going to head on to the next bull riding event. And I saw this out-of-the-way restaurant on the side of road, so I stopped. Next thing I knew, I was here."

Judah shook his head. "A bad hand, man."

"Yeah."

"Never want a woman you've just met to see you weak," Judah mused.

"I wasn't weak. I just got the wrong end of a ride. Or

the flu." Creed glared at Judah. "So anyway, how are the newlyweds? And Fiona? Burke? Everyone else?"

"No one else is getting married, if that's what you're asking. You still have a shot. Like Cinderella getting a glass slipper. It could happen, under the right conditions."

"I don't want a wife or children. That's why I'm here," Creed growled. "You can be the ambassador for both of us, thanks."

"I don't know. I kind of thought that little brunette who went racing out of your room might have some possibilities."

"Then ask her out." Creed felt a headache coming on that had nothing to do with his concussion. It was solely bad temper, which Judah was causing.

Just like the old days. In a way, it was comforting.

"I don't know. I could have sworn I felt that tension thing. You know, a push-pull vibe when she left your room. She was all riled like she had fire on her heels, as if you'd really twisted her up."

"That's a recipe for love if I ever heard one."

"Yeah." Judah warmed to his theory. "Fire and ice. Only she's mostly fire."

"Hellfire is my guess. You know she's a cowboy church preacher."

"Oh." Judah slumped. "That was the fire I picked up on. I knew she needed an extinguisher for some reason. I just thought maybe it had to do with you."

"Nope," Creed said, happy to throw water on his brother's silly theory. "You'll have to hogwash another Callahan into getting roped. And you are not as good as Fiona," Creed warned with satisfaction.

Judah shook his head. "No one is."

"I THINK," FIONA told her friends at the Books 'n' Bingo Society meeting, "that voting a few new members in to our club is a good idea. Sabrina McKinley can't stay shut up in the house all the time taking care of dreadful old Bode Jenkins." Fiona sniffed, despising even saying Bode's name. It was Bode who'd finally closed her up in a trap, and the fact that the man had managed to find a way to get Rancho Diablo from her rankled terribly. She was almost sick with fear over what to tell her six nephews. Pete knew. She could trust Pete. He would keep her secret until the appropriate time. And he was married now, with darling triplet daughters, a dutiful nephew if there ever was one.

But the other five—well, she'd be holding her breath for a long while if she dreamed those five rapscallions would get within ten feet of an altar. No, they'd be more likely to set an altar on fire with their anti-marriage postures. Poof! Up in smoke.

Just like her grip on Rancho Diablo. How disappointed her brother Jeremiah and his wife, Molly, would be if they knew that she'd lost the ranch they'd built. "Some guardian I am," she murmured, and Corrine Abernathy said, "What, Fiona?"

Fiona shook her head. "Anyway, we need to invite Sabrina into our group. We need fresh blood, young voices who can give us new ideas."

Her three best friends and nine other ladies smiled at her benevolently.

"It sounds like a good idea," Mavis Night said. "Who else do you want?"

Fiona thought about it. Sabrina had been an obvious choice for new-member status, because she was Corrine's niece. So was Seton McKinley, a private investigator Fiona had hired to ferret out any chinks in Bode's so-far formidable armor. "I think maybe Bode Jenkins."

An audible gasp went up in the tea room.

"You can't be serious," Nadine Waters said, her voice quavering. "He's your worst enemy."

"And we should keep our enemy close to our bosoms, shouldn't we?" Fiona looked around the room. "Anyway, I put it forth to a vote."

"Why not Sheriff Cartwright? He's a nice man," Nadine offered. "For our first male in the group, I'd rather vote for a gentleman."

Murmurs of agreement greeted that sentiment.

"I don't know," Fiona said. "Maybe I'm losing my touch. Maybe inviting Bode is the wrong idea." She thought about her words before saying slowly, "Maybe I should give up my chairwomanship of the Books 'n' Bingo Society."

Everyone stared at her, their faces puzzled, some glancing anxiously at each other.

"Fiona, is everything all right?" Corinne asked.

"I don't know," Fiona said. She didn't want to tell them that in another six months she might not be here. It was time to lay the groundwork for the next chairwoman. She would have no home which to invite them, there would be no more Rancho Diablo. Only one more Christmas at Diablo. She wanted to prepare her friends for the future. But she also didn't want the truth to come out just yet, for her nephews' sakes. She wanted eligible bachelorettes—the cream of the Diablo crop—to see them still as the powerful Callahan clan, the men who worked the hardest and shepherded the biggest ranch around.

Not as unfortunate nephews of a silly aunt who'd gambled away their birthright.

She wanted to cry, but she wouldn't. "I think I'll adjourn, girls. Why don't we sleep on everything, and next week when we meet maybe we'll have some ideas on forward-thinking goals for our club."

Confused, the ladies rose, hugging each other, glancing with concern at Fiona. Fiona knew she'd dropped a bomb on her friends. She hadn't handled the situation well.

But then, she hadn't handled anything well lately. *I'm definitely losing it,* she thought. In the old days, her most gadabout, confident days, a man like Bode Jenkins would never have gotten the best of her.

She was scared.

"I'M THINKING ABOUT IT," Aberdeen told Johnny that night. "Our nieces need a stable home. And I don't know how to help Diane more than we have. Maybe she needs time away. Maybe she's been through too much. There's no way for us to know what is going through her mind." Aberdeen sat in their cozy upstairs den with Johnny. It was Sunday night so the bar was closed. They'd thoroughly cleaned it after going by to see the recovering cowboy. He'd looked much better and seemed cheered by his brother's presence.

There wasn't much else she and Johnny could do for him, either, and she didn't really want to get any more involved. She had enough on her hands. "Mom and Dad say that they try to help Diane, but despite that, they're afraid the children are going to end up in a foster home somewhere, some day." Aberdeen felt tears press behind her eyelids. "The little girls deserve better than this, Johnny. And Diane has asked me to adopt them. She says she's under too much pressure. Too many children, not enough income, not enough…maternal desire."

That wasn't exactly how Diane had put it. Diane had said she wasn't a fit mother. Aberdeen refused to believe that. Her sister had always been a sunny person, full of optimism. These days, she was darker, moodier, and it all seemed to stem from the birth of her last child. Up until that moment, Diane had thought everything was fine in her marriage. It wasn't until after the baby was born that she'd discovered her husband had another woman. He no longer wanted to be a father, nor a husband to Diane.

"I don't know," Johnny said. "Aberdeen, we live over a bar. I don't think anyone will let us have kids here. Nor could I recommend it. We don't want the girls growing up in an environment that isn't as wholesome as we could make it. We don't even have schools nearby."

Aberdeen nodded. "I know. I've thought about this, Johnny. I think I'm going to have to move to Montana."

Her brother stared at her. "You wanted to leave Montana. So did I."

"But it's not a bad place to live, Johnny." It really wasn't. And the girls would have so much more there than they would living over a bar. "I could be happy there."

"It's not that Montana was the problem," Johnny said. "It was the family tree we wanted to escape."

This was also true. Their parents weren't the most loving, helpful people. They'd pretty much let their kids fend for themselves, believing that they themselves had gotten by with little growing up, and had done fine figuring life out themselves. So Johnny and Aberdeen had left Montana, striking out to "figure life out" on their own. Diane had opted to stay behind with their parents. Consequently, she'd married, had kids, done the wife thing—and left herself no backup when it all fell apart.

"I've been thinking, too," Johnny said. "To be honest, the red flag went up for me when the folks said they were worried. For them to actually worry and not ascribe to their typical let-them-figure-it-out-themselves theory, makes me think the situation is probably dire."

Aberdeen shook her head. "The girls need more. They're so young, Johnny. I don't know exactly what happened to Diane and why she's so determined she can't be a mother anymore, but I think I'm going to either have to get custody or fully adopt, like Diane wants me to do. They need the stability."

Johnny scratched his chin. "We just can't have them here. There are too many strangers for safety."

"That's why I think I have to go to Montana. At least there I can assess what's been happening."

Johnny waved a big hand at her. "Diane is leaving. There's nothing to assess. She's going to follow whatever wind is blowing, and our parents don't want to be bothered with toddlers."

"They don't have the health to do it, Johnny."

"True, but—"

"It doesn't matter," Aberdeen said quickly. "We just need to think of what's best for the girls."

"We can buy a house here. Maybe it's time to do that, anyway."

She looked around their home. It hadn't been in the best condition when they'd bought the building, but they'd converted the large old house into a working/living space that suited them. Upstairs were four bedrooms, with two on either side of an open space, with en suite bathrooms in the two largest bedrooms. They used the wide space between the bedrooms as a family room. For five years they'd lived here, and it was home.

"Maybe," she said, jumping a little when a knock sounded on the front door downstairs. Aberdeen glanced at Johnny. Their friends knew to go to the back door after the bar was closed; they never answered the front door in case a stranger might decide to see if they could get someone to open up the bar. A few drunks over the years had done that. She was surprised when Johnny headed down the stairs. Her brother was big and tall and strong, and he wouldn't open the door without his gun nearby, but still, Aberdeen followed him.

"We're closed," Johnny called through the door.

"I know. I just wanted to come by and say thanks before we left town," a man called from the other side, and Aberdeen's stomach tightened just a fraction.

"The cowboy," she said to Johnny, and he nodded.

"He's harmless enough," Johnny said. "A little bit of a loose cannon, but might as well let him have his say."

Aberdeen shrugged. "He can say it through the door just the same," she said, but Johnny gave her a wry look and opened up.

"Thanks for letting me in," Creed Callahan said to Johnny, shaking his hand as though he was a long-lost friend. "This is the man who probably saved my life, Judah," he said, and Judah put out a hand for Johnny to shake. "Hi, Aberdeen," Creed said.

"Hello, Aberdeen," Judah said, "we met in the hospital."

She smiled at Judah's polite manners, but it was his long-haired ruffian of a brother who held her gaze. She could feel her blood run hot and her frosty facade trying to melt. It was hard not to look at Creed's engaging smile and clear blue eyes without falling just a little bit. *You've been here before,* she reminded herself. *No more bad boys for you.*

"We didn't save your life," Johnny said, "you would have been fine."

Creed shook his head. "I don't remember much about the past couple of days. I don't really recall coming here." He smiled at Aberdeen. "I do remember you telling your brother you didn't want me here."

"That's true." She stared back at him coolly. "We're not really prepared to take in boarders. It's nice to see you on the mend. Will you be heading on now to the next event?"

Judah softly laughed. "We do have to be getting on, but we just wanted to stop by to thank you." He tipped his hat to Aberdeen. "Again, I appreciate you looking out for my brother. He's fortunate to have guardian angels."

Aberdeen didn't feel much like an angel at the moment. She could feel herself in the grip of an attraction unlike anything that had ever hit her before. She'd felt it when she'd first laid eyes on Creed. The feeling hadn't dissipated when she'd visited him in the hospital. She could tell he was one of those men who would make a woman insane from wanting what she couldn't have.

It was the kiss that was muddying her mind. He'd unlocked a desire she'd jealously kept under lock and key, not wanting ever to get hurt again. "Goodbye," she said, her eyes on Creed. "Better luck with your next ride."

He gave her a lingering glance, and Aberdeen could have sworn he had something else he wanted to say but couldn't quite bring himself to say it. He didn't rush to the door, and finally Judah clapped him on the back so he'd get moving toward the exit.

"Goodbye," Creed said again, seemingly only to her, and chicken-heart that she was, Aberdeen turned around and walked upstairs, glad to see him go.

Once in Creed's truck, Judah tried to keep his face straight. Creed knew his brother was laughing at him, though, and it didn't help. "What?" he demanded, pulling out of the asphalt parking lot. "What's so funny?"

"That one is way out of your league, Creed."

Creed started to make a rebuttal of his interest, then shrugged. "I thought you said she'd probably feel responsible for me because she saved me."

Judah laughed. "Works for most guys, clearly backfired on you. Good thing you're not interested in a relationship with a woman, or keeping up with Pete, because you'd never get there if that gal was your choice. I don't believe I've ever seen a female look at a man with less enthusiasm. If you were a cockroach, she'd have squashed you."

He *felt* squashed. "She was like that from the moment I met her," Creed said. "I remember one very clear thing about the night I got here, and that was her big blue eyes staring at me like I was an ex-boyfriend. The kind of ex a woman never wants to lay eyes on again."

"Bad luck for you," Judah said, without much sympathy and with barely hidden laughter. "You're kind of on a roll, bro."

"My luck's bound to turn eventually." Creed was sure it would—he'd always led a fairly charmed existence, but when a man couldn't ride and the ladies weren't biting his well-baited hook and he was evading his wonky little aunt's plan to get him settled down, well, there was

Her mother's gaze was pleading. It occurred to Aberdeen that her sister's mothering skills were basically the same as May's. It was always Johnny who kept the family together, Aberdeen realized. Johnny had been adoring of his little sister and helpful to his big sister and they'd always known they had their protective Johnny looking out for them. Not their parents. Johnny.

"I don't know, Mom," Aberdeen said. "We'd have to see if a court would allow it. We don't know what is involved with an in-family adoption when a mother is simply absent by choice. There's finances to consider, too."

"We can't give you any money," May said quickly, and Johnny said, "We're not asking you for money. We just need to proceed in a responsible fashion for the girls' sakes."

"Well, I would think—" May began, but Johnny cut her off.

"Enough, Mom. We have a lot of decisions to make in the near future. For all we know, Diane could come home next week, ready to be a mother. Maybe she just needed a vacation."

Aberdeen hoped so, but doubted it. "Goodnight," she said, and headed upstairs.

Part of her—the dreamy, irresponsible part she rarely acknowledged—took flight for just an instant, wondering how her life might be different if she, too, just took off, as Diane had, following a man on the whim of her heart.

Like a certain bull rider.

A big, strong, muscular, teasing hunk of six-four cowboy.

But no. She was as different from Diane as night and day. She was a dreamer, maybe, not a doer. She would never fling caution to the wind and follow a man like Creed Callahan.

Yet sweet temptation tugged at her thoughts.

"I've been thinking," Creed told Judah as they made their way through Colorado, "that little cowboy church preacher was a little too uptight for me, anyway."

Judah glanced at him as Creed slumped in the passenger seat, doling out some of their favorite road food. They'd made a pit stop just outside of Denver and loaded up on the junk food Fiona wouldn't allow them to have.

"What made you decide that?" Judah asked, taking a swig of the Big Red Creed had put in the cup holder for him. "Because I was pretty certain uptight might be good for you."

"Maybe in small doses," Creed said, feeling better as every mile took him farther away from temptation. "I'm pretty sure I can't handle uptight in large doses."

"I'd say narrow escape, except I don't think you were in danger of getting caught." Judah munched happily on Doritos from the open bag between the seat. "No, I'm sure you had Free Bird written all over your forehead, bro. No worries."

Creed pondered that. "I've decided to make a run for the ranch."

Judah glanced at him. "Since when?"

Since he'd met the preacher. That was weird, though, Creed thought with a frown. Women usually made him want to get naked, not own a ranch. "I don't know."

"Okay, of all of us, you are not the one to settle down and grow a large family."

"Pete's happy. I could learn by example."

"You ran away from being Pete. Remember? You ran like a hungry wolf to a picnic basket."

Creed considered that as he crunched some chips. "I think I changed when I got my bell rung."

"Creed, you get your bell rung once a year."

"This was different," Creed said. "I saw stars."

"You saw nothing. You weren't yourself for two days," Judah told him. "Anyway, it's not enough to change you. You've always been a loose goose."

"Yeah. I suppose so." Creed lost his appetite for chips and stared morosely at his soda can. "You know, I think Fiona's right. This *is* trash we're eating. I can feel my intestines turning red."

Judah sighed. "This is nectar of the gods."

"Maybe I miss home-cooking. We don't have it bad with Fiona, you know?" The past several months had outlined that to Creed. "We were lucky she raised us."

"Yeah. We could have gone into the system."

"That would have sucked." Creed turned his mind away from thoughts of being separated from his brothers. "Although I met a cowboy who'd been adopted, and he was pretty happy. Things worked out for him."

"It does. But we were in a good place with Fiona and Burke."

"And that's why I intend to fight for the ranch," Creed said with determination. "I just need a woman to help me with this project."

"It'd take you twenty years to *find* a woman," Judah said with some sarcasm, which cut Creed. "I'd say Pete is safe. Anyway, I thought we all agreed that the sacrificial lamb would do the deed, inherit the ranch and divvy it up between all of us. Thereby leaving the rest of us free to graze on the good things in life."

Creed crushed his soda can. "I'm not sure I'm grazing on the good things in life."

"Oh. You want angel food cake." Judah nodded. "Good luck with that. Let me know how it goes, will you?"

Creed rolled his eyes. Judah didn't understand. "I'm just saying, maybe we shouldn't burden Pete with all the responsibility."

"Why not? He's always been the responsible one."

"But maybe some of us should take a crack at being responsible, too. Take the pressure off him. He's got newborn triplets. It's selfish of us to stick him with all the duties."

"I think Fiona's probably realized by now that she can go ahead and award the ranch to Pete. Who could catch up with him? It would take years for one of us to find a woman and then have tons of kids. And what if the woman we found only wanted one? Or none?"

Creed gulped. He tried to envision Aberdeen with a big belly, and failed. She was such a slender woman. He liked slender, but then again, a little baby weight would look good on her. He liked full-figured gals, too.

Hell, he liked them all.

But he'd especially liked her, for some reason.

"It was the thrill of the hunt, nothing more," Judah said, his tone soothing. "Down, boy. It would have come to nothing."

Creed scowled. "I have no idea what you're babbling about."

"We are not settled men by nature. None of us sits and reads a whole lot, for example."

"Not true. Jonas read a hell of a lot to get through

med school. And Sam for law school. And Rafe's been known to pick up a Greek tome or two."

"Pleasure reading. Expand-the-mind reading. That's what I'm talking about."

"Well, we're not reading romance novels, if that's what you're getting at." Creed put away the chips, beginning to feel slightly sick to his stomach. "Although maybe you should."

"What's that supposed to mean?" Judah demanded.

"Maybe if you read romance novels, you'd be able to see that which has been at the end of your nose for years, dummy." Creed jammed his hat down over his eyes, preparing to get in a few winks. "Think about it. It'll come to you." He pondered Judah's thick skull for a moment, then said, "Or maybe not."

Judah made no reply, which was fine with Creed, because all he wanted to do was sit and think about Aberdeen for a few minutes. *Judah is wrong. I owe it to myself to see if I can find a woman I could fall for. I owe it to myself to try to figure out if I'd be a good father. Maybe I would. I like kids.*

Wait. He didn't know that for sure. Truthfully, Pete's babies kind of intimidated him. Of course, they were no bigger than fleas. And fleas weren't good.

Pete's girls were cute as buttons. And they would grow. But they still made him nervous. Maybe he didn't have uncle-type feelings in him. He'd been uninterested in holding them. But they were so small and fragile. *I've eaten breadsticks bigger than their legs.*

Damn. I'm twenty-nine, and I'm scared of my nieces. That can't be good.

"Have you held Pete's kids yet?" Creed asked Judah.

"Nah. They're kind of tiny. And they yell a lot." Judah

shook his head. "I don't want kids. I'm a quiet kind of guy. Organized. Peaceful. Small, squalling things are not peaceful."

Creed felt better. Maybe he wasn't totally a heel for not bonding with his nieces. "I just think I could be good at this, if I put my mind to it."

"At what? Being a dad?" Judah snorted. "Sure. Why not? As long as you give up bull riding and getting dropped on your head, you might be all right."

"Give up bull riding?" Creed echoed, the thought foreign and uncomfortable. He planned on riding until he was a grandfather, if at all possible.. They'd drag him out of the saddle when he was cold and dead and rigor mortis had set in. Cowboy rigor mortis. What man didn't want to die with his boots on?

Of course, if he wasn't good at it anymore... "What the hell am I doing?"

"Search me," Judah replied. "I can't figure you out, bro. It'd take a licensed brain-drainer to do that."

Creed decided not to punch Judah, even though he was pretty certain he should. All he knew was that before his concussion, before he'd met Aberdeen, he'd been sure of who he was. He'd had a plan.

Now, he was asking himself all kinds of questions. Judah was right: It would take a shrink to figure out the knots in his brain.

I should have kissed her again. Then I wouldn't be thinking about her. I'm shallow like that.

I really am.

TWO DAYS LATER, Johnny watched as a man he was particularly displeased to see walked into the bar. This reappearance couldn't have come at a worse time. Johnny was hard to feel bad when as an army of one trying to feel sorry for yourself, you faced an army of five refusing to let you give in to your sorrows. How many times had he and his brothers dug each other out of their foul moods, disappointments or broken hearts?

There weren't as many broken hearts among them as there might have been because they had each other to stall those emotions. When you knew everybody was working too hard to listen to you wheeze, you got over a lot of it on your own. But then, when it was important, you could count on a brother to clout you upside the head and tell you that you were being a candy-ass.

He wasn't at that point yet. "But she's working on me, Bear." He waved his beer at the toy. "I didn't come here to help Johnny. It wasn't the overwhelming reason I said yes, you know? It was her. And then, I got here, and I found out...I found out that maybe I rang my bell so hard that I didn't really pay attention to her when I met her. I think, Bear," he said, lowering his voice to a whisper, "that I have it *bad*."

Really bad, if he was sitting here talking out his woes on a baby's pink bear. Creed sighed, put the bottle on the table and shut his eyes so he wouldn't look at the bear's black button eyes anymore for sympathy he couldn't possibly find. "Grown men don't talk to bears," he said, without opening his eyes, "so if you don't mind, please cease with the chatter so I can get some shut-eye."

If he *could* sleep—without thinking about Aberdeen becoming a mother, a scenario that in no way seemed to have a role for him.

ALL ABERDEEN COULD be when the judge had heard her case was relieved. She was sad for her sister and for her nieces, but it was good to be able to have temporary legal custody of her nieces.

"However," the judge continued, "it's in the best interests of the children that they remain here in Montana, where their maternal grandparents are, and paternal as well, who may be able to provide some assistance."

Shock hit Aberdeen. "Your Honor," she said, "my congregation is in Wyoming. My livelihood is in Wyoming."

The judge looked at her sternly. "A bar isn't much of a place for young, displaced girls to grow up. You have no house for them set apart from the establishment where there could be unsavory elements. And your congregation, as you've described it, is transient. None of this leads me to believe that the situation in Wyoming is more stable for the minors than it would be here, where at least the maternal grandparents can be trusted to oversee the wellbeing of the children."

Aberdeen glanced at Johnny. He would have to go back to Lance. She would be here alone with their parents, who would be little or no help. Tears jumped into Aberdeen's eyes when Johnny clasped her hand. She stared at the judge and nodded her acquiescence.

"Of course, should anything change in your circumstances, the court will be happy to reconsider the situation. Until then, a social worker will be assigned to you." He nodded at Johnny and Aberdeen. "Best of luck to you, Miss Donovan, Mr. Donovan."

Aberdeen turned and walked from the court, not looking at Johnny until they'd gotten outside.

"I expected that," Johnny said, and Aberdeen glanced at him as they walked toward his truck. "That's why I said I'd probably sell the bar. I was hoping it would turn out differently, but I knew Mom and Pop know the judge."

Aberdeen drew in a sharp breath. "Are you saying that they talked to him?"

Johnny climbed in behind the wheel, and Aberdeen got in the passenger side. "I don't know that they did, but I know that he would be familiar with some of our situation. To be fair, any judge hearing this type of case might have decided similarly. But I don't think him knowing Mom and Pop hurt them."

"So now what?" Aberdeen asked.

"Now we're custodians, for the time being," Johnny said. "I've got someone looking for Diane, and if they manage to make contact with her, we'll know a little more. I'll sell the bar, and we'll stay here until matters get straightened out. We're either going to be doing this for the long haul, or it could be as short a time as it takes Diane to come to her senses."

"You don't have to stay here," Aberdeen said. "I've taken this on gladly."

"We're family. We do it together." Johnny turned the truck toward their parents' house.

Aberdeen looked out the window. "I think selling the bar is too drastic, don't you?"

"I can think of more drastic things I don't want to see happen."

Aberdeen looked at him. "I think the worst has already passed."

Her brother took a deep breath, seemed to consider his words. "Look, I just don't want you even starting to think that putting a permanent relationship in your life might be the way to salvage this thing."

"You mean Shawn."

"I mean Re-ride." Johnny nodded. "Don't tell me it hasn't crossed your mind. He as much as admitted to me that he wouldn't be opposed to remarrying you."

Aberdeen shook his head. "He mentioned it. I didn't take him very seriously."

"Stability might start looking good to you after a few months of Mom and Pop interfering with your life."

"So you're selling the bar to move here to protect me from myself?" Aberdeen sent her brother a sharp look. "Johnny, I'm not the same girl I was when Shawn and I got married."

"Look, I don't want to see both my sisters make mistakes is all," Johnny said. "You're not like Diane in any way, but Diane wasn't like this before her marriage fell apart, either."

Aberdeen sighed, reached over to pat Johnny's arm. "I think you worry too much, but thanks for looking out for me. I know you do it out of love and a misguided sense of protection, which I happen to greatly appreciate."

Johnny smiled. "So then. Listen to big brother."

Aberdeen checked her cell phone for messages, then went all in. "Is that why you brought the cowboy back?"

Johnny glanced at her. "I could pretend that I don't know what you're talking about, but I figured you'd suspect, so I might as well just say it doesn't hurt to have an ace in my boot."

"Johnny Donovan," Aberdeen said, "perhaps I'll start meddling in your life. Maybe I'll find a string of cute girls and send them your way to tempt you into matrimony. How would you like that?"

"I hope you do, because I'd like it very much." Johnny grinned. "Make them tall, slender and good cooks. I do love home cooking, and women who want to cook these days are rare."

Aberdeen shook her head. "Creed has no interest in me. And the feeling is mutual. Besides, he wouldn't solve my problem in any way if Diane doesn't come back. Even if he and I got some wild notion to get married, he lives in New Mexico. I don't know that the judge is going to let me take the girls anywhere if you really believe he's influenced by Mom and Pop."

"Still, he'll keep Re-ride busy," Johnny predicted, "and I won't mind that a bit."

"You have a darkly mischievous soul, Johnny," Aberdeen said, but secretly, she had liked seeing Creed Callahan again. It was too bad she and Creed were as opposite as the sun and the moon.

He could make a woman think twice about taking a walk on the *very* wild side.

Chapter Eight

Creed woke up and stretched, hearing birds singing somewhere nearby. It was different here than in Diablo. Everything was different, from the birds to the land, to the—

The pink bear stared at him, and Creed sighed. "Okay, last night won't happen again. You will not be hearing such yak from me again. I had my wheeze, and I'm over it." He carried the bear down to the room where the little girls had been sleeping, and was caught by the sight of tiny dresses, shorts and shoes spread at the foot of a big bed. There were toys scattered everywhere, and even a fragile music box on the dresser top. It was like walking into fairyland, he mused, and he wondered if Aberdeen had had a room like this when she was little.

He backed out of the room after setting the bear on the bed, decided to shower and get cheerful about the day—and there was no better way to get cheerful than to fill his stomach. That would require heading out to the nearest eating establishment, which would be a great way to see Lance. He took a fast shower, jumped into fresh jeans and a shirt, clapped his hat on his head and jerked open the bar door to take in a lungful of fresh, bracing summer air.

Re-ride stared up at him from the ground where he was sitting, leaning against the wall, clearly just awakening.

"Oh, no, this is not going to happen," Creed said, setting the security alarm, locking the door and loping toward his truck. "You and I are not going to be bosom buddies, so buzz off," he called over his shoulder.

Re-ride was in hot pursuit. "Where are you going?" he asked, jumping into the truck when Creed unlocked the door.

"I'm going someplace you're not. Get out." Creed glared at him.

"Breakfast sounds good. I'll show you the hot spots around here." Re-ride grinned. "I know where the best eggs and bacon are in this town."

Creed didn't want the company, but his stomach was growling, and if the eggs were the best… "If you give me any trouble," he said, and Re-ride said, "Nope. Not me."

Creed snorted and followed his new friend's directions to Charity's Diner two streets over. "I'm pretty certain I could have found this place myself," Creed said, and Re-ride laughed.

"But you didn't. Come on. I'll show you some waitresses who are so cute you'll want more than marshmallows in your cocoa."

That made no sense, Creed thought sourly. In fact, it was a pretty stupid remark, but he should probably expect little else from the freeloader. He followed Re-ride into the diner and seated himself in a blue vinyl booth, watching with some amazement as Re-ride waved over a tiny, gorgeous, well-shaped redhead.

"This is Cherry," Re-ride said, "Cherry, this is Creed Callahan."

Creed tipped his hat, noticing that Re-ride's hand fell perilously low on Cherry's nicely curved hip. "Pleasure," he told Cherry, and she beamed at him.

"Cocoa?" she asked Creed.

"Coffee," he said, wary of Re-ride's cocoa promise. "Black as you've got it, please."

She showed sweet dimples and practically stars in her big green eyes as she grinned back at Creed. "Re-ride, you've been hiding this handsome friend of yours. Shame on you."

Re-ride shook his head as he ran his gaze hungrily down a menu, his mind all on food now, though he still clutched Cherry's hip. Creed looked at his own menu as Cherry drifted away, surprised when Re-ride tapped the plastic sheet.

"She likes you, I can tell," Re-ride said.

"Look," Creed said, annoyed, "it's plain that you don't want competition for Aberdeen, but I don't—"

"Oh, there's no competition." Re-ride shook his head. "I told you, I'm marrying Aberdeen. I'm just trying to find you someone, so you won't be odd man out."

Creed sighed. "Odd man out of what? I'm only here for a few days."

"Really?" Re-ride brightened. "I might have misunderstood Johnny when I called him last night."

Creed perked up. "You talked to Johnny?"

"Yep." Re-ride lowered his voice. "You know Aberdeen is trying to adopt Diane's little girls, a horrible idea if there ever was one."

"Why?" Creed asked, telling himself that the Donovan family matters were none of his business, and yet he was so curious he could hardly stand it.

"Because I'm not cut out to be a father," Re-ride explained. "I don't want to be a father to Diane's children."

"Oh." Creed blinked. "Selfish, much?"

"What?" Re-ride glared at him, obviously con-fused.

Creed shrugged. "If you love Aberdeen, wouldn't you want what she wants?"

"No, that's not how it works. I'm the man, and I'll make the decisions about what's best for our family. There's no way a marriage can work when there's no chance for privacy right from the start. A man and his wife need *privacy,* and I'm sure you know what I mean, Callahan."

Fire flamed through Creed's gut. *Jealousy. By God, I'm jealous. I can't be jealous. That would be dumb. But how I wish I could poke this jerk in the nose. I should have beaten him a time or two with that broom handle last night, kind of paying it forward. I sure would feel better now.* "You'd be better off taking that up with Aberdeen than with me," Creed said, keeping his tone mild even as his heart had kicked into overdrive. Maybe he was getting a mild case of indigestion. His whole chest seemed to be enduring one large attack of acid.

"You paying, cowboy?" Re-ride asked. "I'm short a few at the moment."

He was short more things than dollars, but Creed just shook his head, deciding it wouldn't kill him to help out the poor excuse for a man. "I suppose," he said, and Re-ride proceeded to call Cherry back over to give her a list of items that would have fed an army.

Creed sighed to himself. If anyone had ever told him he'd be buying breakfast for the ex-husband and current suitor of a woman that Creed had a small crush on, he would have said they were crazy.

"Turns out I'm the crazy one," he muttered, and Re-ride said, "Yeah, I heard that about you."

Creed drank his coffee in silence.

WHEN CREED AND his unwanted companion returned to Johnny's bar, Creed said, "Sayonara, dude," and Re-ride hurried after him.

"No," Creed said, shutting the door in Re-ride's face.

"This isn't how you treat friends!" Re-ride called through the door.

"Exactly," Creed said, turning to study the bar. He decided he'd go upstairs and call his brothers, see how the old homestead was doing. He'd only been gone a day and a half—not much could have changed in his absence. He got out his laptop, too, to surf while he chatted. "This is the life," he said, making himself comfortable in the den. He ignored the banging on the door downstairs. Re-ride would go away soon, or he'd fall asleep outside the door again, and either way, it wasn't Creed's problem.

Until Aberdeen came back. Then Re-ride's constant presence would be a problem.

Yet, no. It couldn't be. Aberdeen was nothing to him, and he was nothing to her, and he was only here to pay back a favor. Not get involved in their personal family business.

Or to fall for her.

"That's right. I'm not doing that," he said, stabbing numbers into the cell phone. Re-ride had ceased banging for the moment, which was considerate of him.

"Howdy, Aunt Fiona," he said, when his aunt picked up, and she said, "Well, fancy you calling right now, stranger."

"What does that mean?" Creed's antennae went

straight up at his aunt's happy tone. Aunt Fiona was never happier than when she was plotting, but surely he hadn't been gone long enough for her to have sprung any plots.

"It means that you must have telekinetic abilities. We just mailed out the invitations to the First Annual Rancho Diablo Charity Matchmaking Ball!"

Creed blinked. "That's a mouthful, Aunt."

"It is indeed. And we are going to have mouthfuls of food, and drink and kissing booths—"

"I thought—" He didn't want to hurt Aunt Fiona's feelings, so he chose his words carefully. "Why are we having a…what did you call it again?"

"A First Annual Rancho Diablo Charity Matchmaking Ball!" Aunt Fiona giggled like a teenage girl. "Doesn't it sound like fun? And it's all Jonas's idea!"

Creed's brows shot up. He could feel a headache starting under his hatband, so he shucked his hat and leaned back in Johnny's chair. Outside the window ledge, a familiar face popped into view.

"Let me in!" Re-ride mouthed through the window, and Creed rolled his eyes.

"Get down before you kill yourself, dummy," he said loudly, and Aunt Fiona said,

"Why, Creed! How could you speak to me that way?"

"No, Aunt. I'm not—" He glared at Re-ride and headed into another room. It was Aberdeen's room, he realized with a shock, and it carried her scent, soft and sweet and comforting. Sexy. And holy Christmas, she'd left a nightie on the bed. A white, lacy nightie, crisp white sheets, fluffy pillows…a man could lie down on that bed and never want to get up—especially if he was holding her.

But he wasn't. Creed gulped, taking a seat at the vanity instead so he could turn his face from the alluring nightie and the comfy bed which beckoned. It was hard to look away. He had a full stomach, and a trainload of desire, and if he weren't the chivalrous man that he was, he'd sneak into that bed and have a nap and maybe an erotic dream or two about her. "When is this dance, Aunt?"

"Be home in two weeks," she commanded, her typical General-Fiona self. "We're rushing this because Jonas says we must. I wanted to have it in a month, when I could order in something more fancy than barbecue, but Jonas says time is of the essence. We need ladies here fast. Well, he didn't say that, but that's the gist of it."

Creed sighed. "None of us dance, Aunt Fiona. You know that."

"I know. I never saw so many men with two left feet. Fortunately," Aunt Fiona went on, "you still draw the ladies in spite of your shortcomings. My friends have put out the calls, and we've already had a hundred responses in the affirmative. This should be a roaring success in the social columns, I must say!"

This didn't sound like one of Jonas's plans. "I've only been gone a few hours," Creed said, reeling, and Aunt Fiona snapped,

"We didn't have time to wait on you to get back here, Creed, and heaven knows you're not one for making fast decisions. But Jonas is. And he is light on his feet when it comes to planning. I have great hopes for him."

Creed said to hell with it and moved to Aberdeen's bed, testing it out with a gentle bounce. It was just as soft and comfortable as it looked. "I'm afraid to ask, but why do we need a charity ball?"

"To get your brothers married, of course. And you, but I think you'll be the last to go." Fiona sounded depressed about that. "You're still haring around, trying to figure out what you want in life, Creed."

Right now he wanted a nap in this sweet bed. Telling himself he was a fool to do it—he was treading into dangerous territory—Creed picked up the lacy white nightie with one finger, delicately, as though the sheer lace might explode if he snagged it with his work-roughened hands. "I know what I want in life, Aunt Fiona," he said softly, realizing that maybe he did know, maybe he'd known it from the moment he'd met her, but there were too many things in the way that he couldn't solve. His aunt was right—he was still going after something he couldn't have. "What are we wearing to this shindig, anyway?"

"Whatever you want to wear," Aunt Fiona said, "but I'll warn you of this. Your brothers are going all out in matching black tuxes. Super-formal, super-James Bond. They intend to dance the night away and seduce the ladies in ways they've never been seduced."

Creed stared at the nightgown, seduced already. But what good would it do? There was an eager ex-husband jumping around outside, climbing to second-story windowsills, trying to make himself at home. And Creed was feeding him. "Sounds like fun, Aunt Fiona," he said. "Guess I'll shine up my best boots."

"I'll just be grateful if you get here and ask a lady to dance," Aunt Fiona said, "so hurry home."

"Don't worry. I'll be home very soon."

"You promise?"

"I swear I do."

"Then I hold you to that. I love you, even though you

are a wily coyote. I must go now, Jonas is yelling at me to buy more stamps for the invitations. He had them made special in town, and then printed invitations in all the nearby papers. I tell you, your brother's a magician. I don't know why I didn't notice it before."

She hung up. Creed stared at his cell for a moment, finally turning it off. He was dumbfounded, in a word. Aunt Fiona must have worked a heck of a spell on Jonas to put him in such a partying mood. Jonas was not the ladies' man in the family. Nor did he have the most out-going disposition. Creed frowned. There was something off about the whole thing, but it was Aunt Fiona and her chicanery, so "off" was to be expected.

Still, it made him tired. Or maybe Re-ride had made him tired. It didn't matter. He'd slept on the sofa last night, and he hadn't slept well, and the eggs had filled him up, and Re-ride was quiet for the moment, so Creed took one last longing look at the white lace nightie he held in his hand, and leaned back against the padded headboard just for a second.

Just for a quick moment to see what it would feel like to sleep in Aberdeen's bed. A guy could dream— couldn't he?

His eyes drifted closed.

CREED HAD NEVER slept so hard. Never slept so well. It was as though he was enclosed in angel wings, dream-ing the peaceful dreams of newborn babies. He didn't ever want to wake up. He knew he didn't want to wake up because he was finally holding Aberdeen in his arms. And she was wearing the hot nightie, which was short enough and sheer enough not to be a nightie at all. He'd died and gone to heaven. Everything he'd ever wanted was in his arms.

He heard a gasp, and that wasn't right; in his dreams, everyone was supposed to make happy, soft coos of delight and admiration. Creed's eyes jerked open to find Aberdeen staring at him—and Re-ride.

It was a horrible and rude awakening. There was no hope that he wouldn't look like some kind of pervert, so Creed slowly sat up. He removed the nightie from his grasp and shoved it under a pillow so Re-ride couldn't get more of a glimpse of it than necessary. "Hi, Aberdeen. Did everything go well?"

"Yes." She crossed her arms, glaring at him. "Shawn says you've been running all over town, not watching the bar at all. He says he had to come in and look after it last night because he thought he saw a prowler!"

Creed flicked a glance at Re-ride. The traitor stared back at him, completely unashamed of his sidewinder antics. "Did he say that?" Creed asked, his voice soft, and Aberdeen nodded vigorously.

"And may I ask why you're in my bed?"

It was a fair question, and one to which he didn't have a good answer. And he was already in the dog house. Creed sighed. "You can ask, but I don't have a good reason."

"Then will you get out of it?" Aberdeen said, and Creed got to his feet.

"I guess I'll be going." He walked to the door, glancing back only once, just in time to see Re-ride grab Aberdeen and give her the kind of kiss a man gives a woman when he's about to emblazon her hand with a diamond ring fit for a princess. Creed could hear wedding bells tolling, and it hurt.

All his dreams—stupid dreams—were shot to dust. He slunk down the hallway, telling himself he'd been an idiot ever to have trusted Re-ride. "That yellow-bellied coward. I live with Aunt Fiona and five brothers. How could I have let myself be gamed like that?" Creed grabbed up his laptop and his few belongings, and five minutes later he was heading down the stairs, his heart heavy, feeling low.

Re-ride went running past him, hauling ass for the front door. He jetted out of the bar, running toward town. Creed hesitated in the doorway, wondering if he should check on Aberdeen.

She came down the stairs, lifting her chin when she saw him. "You're still here?"

Creed blinked. "Re-ride just beat me to the door, or I'd be gone already."

She had enough ice in her eyes to freeze him, and Creed was feeling miserably cold already.

"Why were you in my bed?"

"I fell asleep. Is that a crime? It's not like I was Goldilocks and I tried out all the beds in the house and thought yours was the best. Although from my random and incomplete survey, so far it is pretty nice."

"I wasn't expecting to find you in my bed."

"I wasn't actually expecting to be in it, it just happened that way," he said with some heat, still smarting that Re-ride had painted him in a thoroughly unflattering light, and liking it even less that Aberdeen had believed the worst of him. Women! Who needed them? "I went in there, I fell asleep. End of story. And I'm not sorry," he said, "because it was damn comfortable, and I slept like a baby. Frankly, I was beat."

She looked at him for a long moment. "Would you

like to sleep all night in my bed?" she asked, and Creed's pulse rocketed. Women didn't say something like that unless they meant something awesome and naked, did they?

"I should probably be hitting the road," Creed said, not sure where he stood at the moment, although the direction of the conversation was decidedly more optimistic than it had been a few moments ago.

She nodded. "Okay. I understand."

He understood nothing at all. "Understand what?"

She shrugged. "Thanks for watching the bar, Creed. And I'm sorry for what I said. I should have known better than to believe anything Shawn says."

"You mean Re-ride?" Creed glanced over his shoulder to see if the cowboy had reappeared, but there was a dust plume from the man's exit. "What changed your mind?"

"He proposed," she said simply. "And I realized he was doing it because of you."

"Yeah, well. I have that effect on men, I guess. They get jealous of me because it's obvious the ladies prefer me." Creed threw in a token boast to boost his self-esteem. Aberdeen had him tied in a cowboy's knot.

"So," Aberdeen slowly said, "the offer's still open if you're not of a mind to hit the road just yet."

Creed hung in the doorway, feeling as if something was going on he didn't quite understand, but he wasn't about to say no if she was offering what he thought she was. Still, he hesitated, because he knew too well that Aberdeen wasn't the kind of woman who shared her bed with just anyone. "Where's Johnny? And the little girls?"

"They're in Spring, Montana. I just came back to get some of our things." Aberdeen looked at him, her eyes shy, melting his heart. "And then I'll be going back."

She wasn't telling everything, but Creed got that she was saying she wouldn't be around. And she'd just told Re-ride to shove off, so that meant—

He hardly dared to hope.

Until she walked to him, leaned up on her toes, and pressed her lips against his.

And then he allowed himself to hope.

Chapter Nine

The first thing Creed noticed about Aberdeen was that she was a serious kisser. There was no shyness, no holding back. When he pulled her close and tight, she melted against him.

That was just the way he wanted her. Yet Creed told himself to go slow, be patient. She'd been married to quite the dunderhead; Creed wanted to come off suave, polished. Worthy of her. He would never get his fill of her lips, he decided, knowing at once that Cupid's arrow had shot him straight through.

She only pulled back from him once, and stared up into his eyes. "Are you sure about this?"

He gulped. That was usually the man's question, wasn't it? And here she was asking him like he was some shy lad about to lose his virginity. "I've never been more sure of anything in my life."

"Then lock the door, cowboy. Bar's closed for the rest of the day. And night."

He hurriedly complied, and then she took his hand, leading him upstairs. Creed's heart was banging against his ribs; his blood pressure was through the roof. *Let this be real, and not that horny dream I'd promised myself.* When Aberdeen locked the bedroom door behind them, he knew he was the luckiest man on earth. "Come here," he told her, "let me kiss you."

If he had the whole night, then he was going to kiss her for hours. He took her chin gently between his palms, his lips meeting hers, molding against her mouth. She moaned and he was happy to hear that feminine signal, so he turned up the heat a notch. She surprised him by eagerly undoing his shirt buttons, never taking her lips from his until she had his shirt completely undone. Then she pulled away for just a moment, her hands slipping his shirt off, her gaze roaming over his chest, her hands greedily feeling the tight muscles of his stomach and the knotted cords of his shoulders.

She looked as though she was starving for love and affection. He'd never made love to a preacher lady, but he'd figured she would have all kinds of hang-ups and maybe a go-slow button. Aberdeen acted as if he was some kind of dessert she'd promised herself after a month-long fast. And he didn't want to get drawn in to any lingering firefight between her and Re-ride, if that was what was going on here. He caught her hands between his, pressing a kiss to her palms. "Aberdeen, is everything all right?"

She nodded up at him, her eyes huge. "Yes."

"You're sure you want this?"

She nodded again. "Yes, I do, and if you don't quit being so slow, I'm going to be forced to drag you into my bed, Creed."

Well, that was it. A man could only play the firefighter so long when he really wanted to be the raging fire. So he picked her up and carried her to her white bed, laying her gently down into the softness. Slowly, he took off her sandals, massaging each delicate ankle.

He unbuttoned her sundress, every white button down the front of the blue fabric, patiently, though it seemed to take a year and he wasn't certain why a woman needed so many buttons. He kissed her neck, keeping her still against the bed, his shoulders arched over her body, and still she kept pulling him toward her. In fact, she was trying to get his jeans off, and doing a better job of it than he was doing with the dress, but Creed was determined to have her out of her clothes first and lavish on her the attention he'd been so hungry to give her. Slipping the dress to the floor, he moved Aberdeen's hands to her side and murmured, "Don't worry. I'm going to take good care of you," and she sighed as though a ton of burdens had just slid off her. He slipped off her bra, delighted by the tiny freckles on her breasts, which, he noticed, happened to match the same sprinkles on her thighs. He took his time kissing each freckle, then slowly slipped a nipple into his mouth, tweaking the other with his hand. She moaned and arched against him, but he pressed her against the sheets again, keeping her right where he wanted her.

"Slow," Creed murmured against Aberdeen's mouth. "I'm going to take you very slowly."

She tried to pull him toward her, but there wasn't any way he was going to be rushed. He captured her hands in one of his, keeping them over her head so he could suck on her nipples, lick her breasts, tease her into readiness. Every inch of her was a treasure he'd been denied for so long; he just wanted to explore everything, leave nothing behind. She was twisting against him, her passion growing, and he liked knowing that she was a buttoned-up lady for everyone else but him. He let her hands go free so that he could cup a breast with one hand, shucking his boots with the other, and then started the heavenly trail down her stomach.

There were cute freckles there, too. Aberdeen gasped, her fingers tangling in his hair. He could feel her control completely slipping, which was the way he wanted her, wild with passion. Looping his fingers in the sides of her panties, he pulled them down, bit by bit revealing the hidden treasure.

And there was nothing he could do once he saw all of Aberdeen's beauty but kiss her in her most feminine place. She went still, surprised, he thought, but he had more surprises in store for her. She was too feminine to resist, and he'd waited too long. Her body seemed made for his; she felt right, she fitted him, and he couldn't stand it any longer. He slipped his tongue inside her— and Aberdeen cried out. He spread her legs apart, moving to kiss those pin-sized freckles on her thighs, but she buried her hands in his hair again, and it sure seemed like begging to him, so Creed obliged. He kissed her, and licked her, holding her back, knowing just how close he could get her before she exploded, and then, knowing she was too ladylike to beg—next time, he'd make sure he got her to totally let go—he put a finger inside her, massaging her while he teased her with his tongue.

Aberdeen practically came apart in his hands.

"Creed!" she cried, pulling at him desperately, and he fished a condom out of his wallet, putting it on in record time. Holding her tightly, he murmured, "Hang on," and kissing her, slid inside her.

She felt like heaven. This *was* heaven. "If I do this every day for the rest of my life, it won't be enough," he whispered against her neck, and when Aberdeen stiffened in his arms, he moved inside her, tantalizing her, keeping her on edge. She was holding back in spirit, in her heart, but as Creed brought her to a crying-out-loud climax, he kissed her, thinking she had no clue that she couldn't run him off as easily as she'd run off Re-ride. He just wasn't that kind of shallow.

"Aberdeen," he murmured, his mind clouding, nature taking over his body. He'd only pleasured her twice, but he couldn't stand it any longer. He rode her into the sheets, the pressure commanding him to possess her, never give her up, take her to be his. She cried out, grabbing his shoulders, locking her legs around him, crying his name, surrendering this much passion, he knew, against her will. When he came, he slumped against her, breathing great gulps of air, and murmured her name again. It was engraved in his heart.

Aberdeen just didn't know that yet. She'd be hard to convince. She'd have a thousand reasons why they couldn't be together.

But if he knew anything at all, if he understood one thing about his destiny, it was that Aberdeen Donovan was meant to be his by the glorious hand of Fate.

And he was damned grateful.

ABERDEEN LAY UNDERNEATH Creed practically in shock. Never in her life had she experienced anything like that. She hadn't even known making love could be such… so much fun, for one thing. If you could call that fun. She felt as if she'd had her soul sucked from her and put back better.

She wiggled, trying to see if he had fallen asleep on her. Her eyes went wide. Was he getting hard again? It certainly felt like he was. He was the hardest man she'd ever felt, like steel that possessed her magically. All she had for comparison was Re-ride, and that wasn't much of a comparison. Aberdeen bit her lip as that thought flew right out of her brain. Creed *was* getting hard inside her again! She'd figured he'd want her once and go on his way, the way her ex had—and then she'd pack the things she needed and head to Montana.

He wouldn't miss her—he wasn't that kind of guy. He probably had women in every town. So she hadn't felt too guilty about seducing him. She'd just wanted a little pleasure, something for herself, an answer to the question she'd had ever since she'd seen his admiration for her burning in his navy gaze. He was too good-looking and too much of a rascal—a bad boy a woman fantasized about—for her not to want the question answered. She wasn't an angel. And right now she was glad of that, because he was hard, and he wanted her, and even if she hadn't planned on making love to Creed twice, she wasn't about to say no.

Not after the pleasure he'd just given her.

He looked deep into her eyes, not saying a word. She didn't know what to say to him. He made all the words she ever thought she might say just dry up. He made a lazy circle around one of her breasts, and she could feel him getting even harder inside her. He kissed her lips, sweetly and slowly, and Aberdeen's breath caught somewhere inside her chest.

To her surprise, he rolled her over on her stomach, and she went, trusting him. He reached for another condom, and kissed her shoulders, as if he wanted to calm her, soothe her. So she waited with held breath as he kissed down her spine, finding points which seemed to intrigue him. He kissed her bottom reverently, took a nip here and there, licked the curve of her hips.

And then the hardness filled her again as he slid inside her. She tried not to cry out, but oh, she couldn't stop herself. He held her gently, not demanding, not passionate and eager as he'd been before, and he rocked her against him, filling her with him. He tweaked a breast, rolling it between his fingers as he kissed her neck, and she couldn't stop her body from arching back against him. She didn't know exactly what she wanted, but when he put a hand between her legs, teasing her, the combination of steel and gentle teasing sent her over the edge again. "Creed," she said on a gasp, and he said, "Say it again," against her neck, and she obeyed him as he drove her to another climax. And when she said his name a third time—she heard herself scream it—he pounded inside her, taking her until his arms tightened around her and his body collapsed against hers.

But still he didn't let her go.

And now, she didn't want him to.

WHEN ABERDEEN AWAKENED, Creed wasn't in her bed. She rose, glancing around the room, listening.

There was nothing to hear.

He'd left. He'd gone back to New Mexico. Her heart racing, Aberdeen crawled from the sheets, sore in places she couldn't remember being sore before. And yet it felt good, a reminder of the passion she'd finally experienced.

No wonder the Callahans were famous. She peeked out the window, but his truck was gone. Her heart sank, though she'd expected him to head off. Men like Creed didn't hang around. Hadn't she learned that from Shawn? Oh, he'd come back in the end, but he hadn't really wanted her. She'd figured that out quick enough when Shawn proposed to her.

She'd told him she had custody of her nieces, and he'd told her he didn't want to be a father. That had inflamed her, and she'd told Shawn that if he didn't get out of her room, out of her house, she'd set Creed on him.

Those were the magic words. Her ex had run as though devils were on his tail.

Aberdeen got into the shower, thinking she had a lot to be grateful to the Callahan cowboy for. She'd known there was no future for the two of them—there were too many differences in their lives—but still, she wished he'd said goodbye.

She took a long shower, letting the hot water calm her mind. She didn't want to think about her nieces at the moment, or custody, or cowboys she couldn't have. Raspberry body wash—her favorite—washed all the negative thoughts away, and she grabbed a white towel to wrap around her body and began to dry her hair. If she hurried, she could leave in an hour. She'd close up the bar, put on the security alarm, and drive to the next phase in her life. She doubted she'd ever see Creed again. A tiny splinter of her heart broke off, and she told herself she was being silly. Just because she'd slept with him, that didn't mean they could be anything to each other. But still, she'd started to think of him as someone in her life—

She heard the door downstairs open and close. Her pulse jumped. Creed had left, but surely he'd locked the door. She'd seen the closed sign in the window when they'd come home.

Boots sounded on the stairs. Aberdeen froze, holding her towel tightly around her. She could hardly hear for the blood pulsing in her ears.

When Creed walked into the room, her breath didn't release, as it should have, with relief. If anything, she was even more nervous. "I thought you'd gone."

He smiled at her. He'd showered, but he must have used Johnny's room, which made sense. His longish hair was slightly wet at the ends. His dark-blue eyes crinkled at the sides.

"Did you dress for me, Aberdeen?" he asked, his voice a teasing drawl.

Blush heated her face. She decided to brave this out. "As I said, I thought you'd gone."

He nodded. "I didn't want to wake you up when I went out. You were sleeping like a princess."

Of course he was well aware he'd made her feel like a princess. Her defenses went up. "Why are you here?"

His gaze swept her toes, up her calves, considered the towel she clutched before returning to her face. He gave her a smile only a rogue would wear. "Do you want me to leave?"

She wanted him, and he knew it. He was toying with her. "I don't know why I would want you here," she said, "I'm leaving today, and I'm sure you have places to go."

He took off his hat and laid it on her vanity. Her heart jumped inside her, betraying her inner feelings. "I do have places to go, things to do," he agreed.

She didn't trust the gleam in his eyes. Tugging the towel tighter against her, she lifted her chin. "Where did you go?"

"Out for a little while."

He didn't move closer, so Aberdeen felt on firm footing. "Did you come back to say goodbye? Because if you did, you can say it and go. No guilt." She took a deep breath. "I know you have a long drive."

He nodded. "I do."

She waited, her heart in a knot, too shy suddenly to tell him she wished everything could be different—

"I didn't come back to say goodbye," he said, stepping toward her now. "You need breakfast before you leave, and I need you."

She stood her ground as he came near, and when he reached out and took hold of the towel, she allowed him to take it from her body. He dropped it to the floor, his gaze roaming over her as if he'd never seen her body before. He seemed to like what he saw. He took her face in his hands, kissing her lips, her neck, and Aberdeen closed her eyes, letting her fingers wander into his hair as he moved to her stomach, kissing lower until he licked inside her, gently laving all the sore places until they felt healed and ready for him again. She moaned, her knees buckling, her legs parting for him, and when Creed took her back to her bed, laying her down, Aberdeen told herself that one more time enjoying this cowboy in her bed was something she deserved. She couldn't have said no if her life had depended on it. He made her feel things she'd never felt before, and she wanted to feel those things again, and he knew it.

He took out a new box of condoms. Aberdeen watched him, wanting to say that he wasn't going to need an entire new box since they both had places to be—but by the time he'd undressed and gotten into bed with her, murmuring sweet things against her stomach, telling her she was a goddess, Aberdeen slid her legs apart and begged him to come to her. And when Creed did, she held him as tightly as she could, rocking against him until she felt him get stronger and then come apart in her arms, which somehow felt better even than anything he'd done to her.

She was in heaven in his arms—and she didn't want to be anywhere else.

Chapter Ten

Time seemed to stand still for Creed, suspended between what he wanted and what was realistic. The sleeping woman he held in his arms was what he wanted. Realistically, winning her was going to be hard to achieve.

He had to give it everything in his power. There were a hundred reasons he could think of that Aberdeen had to be his—but convincing her would take some serious effort.

It would be worth it, if he could convince her.

He realized she was watching him. "Hello, beautiful," he said, stroking her hair away from her face.

She lowered her lashes. He liked her a little on the shy side; he enjoyed tweaking her, too. She was so cute, tried so hard to be reserved, and then she was all eager and welcoming in bed. "I want you again," he told her. "I don't know how you have this spell on me."

She stroked a hand over his chest. He kissed the tip of her nose, and then lightly bit it. She pinched his stomach, just a nip, and he grinned at her, giving her bottom a light spank. She jumped, her eyes wide, and he laughed, holding her tighter against him. "I could stay here with you for weeks, just making love to you. I don't even have to eat."

He would just consume her. He kissed her lips, taking his sweet time to enjoy that which he'd wanted for so long.

"I have to go, Creed," Aberdeen said, "as much as I would love to stay here with you."

He grunted, not about to let her go this moment. There was too much he still needed to know. "What happened to Re-ride? Why did he take off?"

She gazed at him, and Creed couldn't resist the pain in her eyes, so he kissed her lips, willing her to forget the pain and think only of the pleasure he could give her.

"He got cold feet," Aberdeen said.

"How cold?"

"Ice." She looked at him. "Arctic."

"He said he was going to marry you again." Creed palmed her buttocks, holding her close against him so he could nuzzle her neck, feel her thighs against his. She slipped a thigh between his, and he nearly sighed with pleasure. She was so sweet, so accommodating. He really liked that about her.

"He talks big." Aberdeen laid her head against his shoulder, almost a trusting, intimate gesture, and Creed liked that, too. "He didn't want me to adopt the girls, but I am going to, if I have to. If it's the right thing for them. If my sister, Diane, doesn't come back, then I'll move to the next phase. Right now, I've been awarded temporary custody. Shawn wanted to be part of my life, so he claimed, knew I was going to adopt my nieces if I had to, but when I told him I had to move to Montana, he went cold." She ran a palm lightly over his chest. "I told him if he didn't get out, you'd throw him out. Or something to that effect. I hope you don't mind."

Creed grinned, his chin resting on top of Aberdeen's head. "I never miss a chance to be a hero."

"So that's my story. What's yours?"

Creed thought his story was too long and too boring to bother anyone with. He didn't want to talk about it anyway. "I don't have a story."

Aberdeen pulled away. "That's dirty pool. You can't pull out my story, and then keep yours to yourself."

She had a point. He pushed her head back under his chin and gave her another light paddling on the backside. "Have I ever told you I don't like opinionated women?"

She made a deliberately unappreciative sound which he would call a snort. "I like my women a little more on the obedient side," he said, teasing her, enjoying trying to get her goat, only because he wanted to see what her retribution would be. He liked her spicy. Spice was good.

"I like my men a little more on the honest side," Aberdeen shot back, and Creed smiled to himself.

"That's my sweet girl," he said, and Aberdeen gave him a tiny whack on his own backside, surprising him. He hadn't expected her to turn the tables on him.

"So, your story?" Aberdeen prompted.

"I need to get married," Creed said, his gaze fixed on the vanity across the room as he thought about his life in New Mexico. "My aunt wants all of us to get married."

Aberdeen pulled away from him to look into his eyes. "And do you have a prospect back in New Mexico?"

"No," he said, pulling her back against him, "I don't. So my aunt—who is a formidable woman—is planning a marital ball of some kind to introduce me and my four unmarried brothers to eligible ladies."

"Why does your aunt care if you're unmarried or not?"

"Because she's bossy like that." Creed loved the smell of Aberdeen's shampoo. Raspberry or strawberry—something clean and fresh and feminine. He took a deep breath, enjoying holding her. "And the women she'll have at the ball will be highly eligible. Socially acceptable. Drop-dead gorgeous."

"So what are you doing here?" Aberdeen asked, and Creed grinned, fancying he heard just a little bite in her words.

"Sleeping with you? Oh, this is just a fling." He kissed her lips, though she tried to evade him. "Didn't you say that you had to leave for Montana? So you're just having a little fun before you go back. I understand that. Men do it all the time." He sucked one of her nipples into his mouth, and Aberdeen went still, though she'd been trying to move to the edge of the bed, putting room between them.

"I don't know what this is," Aberdeen said, and he heard honesty in her voice. He released her nipple and kissed her on the mouth instead.

"You were going to say yes to Re-ride."

She looked at him, her gaze clear. "I hate to admit that I briefly considered it."

"But it didn't work out before."

She shook her head. "I suppose I was desperate enough to wonder if it might have been the best idea."

He hated the sound of that. "Because of your nieces?"

"I only have temporary custody. The judge didn't seem to find me all that compelling as a guardian. I feel like I need more stability in my life to convince him. He pointed out that Johnny and I live over a bar, not exactly suitable for children. The clientele is transient. He doesn't know Johnny and me. He does know our parents, and made the assumption that they'll be available to help us out. What he didn't understand is that our parents didn't even raise us." Aberdeen seemed ashamed to admit this, and Creed put his chin on her shoulder again, holding her tight. "So I can't leave Montana with the kids. I think if my marital status were to change, that would be something in my favor."

"And along came Re-ride, and you saw your prince."

Aberdeen shrugged. "It made sense at the time."

Creed could see the whole picture. He understood now why Johnny had called him to come watch the bar. Johnny didn't like Re-ride. Johnny had called Creed in, hoping Creed might have an eye for his sister.

"Tell me something," Creed said, "why are you here to get your things instead of Johnny?"

"Johnny was going to come, and I was going to stay with the girls. But then Johnny said he thought it would be better if he stayed because our folks give him a little less trouble. Very few people bother Johnny. He's always been my biggest supporter."

"Protective big brother," Creed murmured, and Aberdeen said, "Yes."

And so Creed had run off the competition, just as Johnny had probably hoped. Creed could spot a plot a mile away, even if he was late to figure it out. Fiona had given him good training. He tipped her chin back with a finger. "Preacher lady, you need a husband, and it just so happens I need a wife."

She blinked. Seemed speechless. Her eyes widened, like she thought he was joking. He kissed her hand, lightly bit the tip of a finger before drawing it into his mouth. She pulled her finger away, then glared at him.

"That's not funny."

"I'm not joking." Creed shrugged.

"You're serious."

"Men don't joke about marriage." Creed shook his head. "It's a very serious matter worthy of hours of cogitation."

"Are you suggesting we have some sort of fake marriage? To fool the judge and to fool your aunt?"

"*Fooling*'s kind of a harsh word." Creed kissed her neck, ignoring her when she tried to push him away. She couldn't; he outweighed her by a hundred pounds, and he sensed she wasn't serious about moving him away from her delightful body. She just needed distance while her mind sorted the conclusion he'd already come to. "I'm just suggesting we become a stable, responsible married couple for all interested parties."

"You want to marry me just to get your aunt off your back?"

Creed laughed. "You make it sound so simple. Aunt Fiona is not that easy to fool. You'll have to be a very enthusiastic bride. Or she'll find me a better wife."

Aberdeen shook her head. "It's a silly reason to get married. I counsel people on making proper decisions regarding marriage vows. This would be a sham."

"*Sham* is also a harsh word." He kissed the tip of her nose. "I prefer *happy facade.*"

Her glare returned. "*Happy facade* sounds ridiculous. Marriage should be a contract between two people who trust each other."

"Think of all the benefits. I'd sleep with you every night, Aberdeen. I promise." He tugged her up against him, so he could kiss between her breasts. "We're a good fit in bed."

"Sex isn't enough." Aberdeen tried to squirm away.

"It's not enough, but it sure is a lot." He rolled her over so he could spoon against her back and nip her shoulder lightly at the same time. "Good thing you like sex as much as you do. I wouldn't want a frigid wife."

She gasped and tried to jump out of the bed. "Aberdeen, you know you like it. Don't try to deny it." He laughed and tugged her against him. "Were you reaching for the condoms, love? If you hand me a couple, I'll give you an hour you'll never forget."

She went still in the bed. He held her against him, stroking her hips, letting her decide if she was going to be angry with him or take the bait. Either way, he had a plan for that.

"You're too crazy for me to marry," Aberdeen said, "even if you're serious, which I don't think you are."

"I'm as serious as a heart attack, love."

She flipped over to stare into his eyes. "Where would we live?"

"In my house in New Mexico. Wherever that's going to be."

"A house?" He could feel her taste the words, and realized having a house was a dream of hers.

"Mmm," he murmured, unable to resist running a palm down her breasts. "House, yard, school nearby, church, the works. Nothing fancy. But a home."

"Why would you be willing to have my three nieces live with you?" She looked as though she didn't quite believe what she was hearing.

He shrugged. "I don't mind kids. They didn't exactly run screaming from me, and I thought that was a good start. And my aunt wants us to have as many children as possible."

She crooked a brow. "Can't you have your own?"

He laughed. "Come here and let's find out."

Aberdeen squirmed away, studying his face. "Men don't get married and take on other people's children because of aunts."

"Probably not." He could feel her brain whirring a mile a minute, trying to find the trap. She didn't get it, and even if he told her, she wouldn't believe him. *I like her, I honestly like her. I like her body. I like her innocence. I think she'd like being married to me. That's as much as I know about why people get married anyway. This feels good and real, when it's always felt kind of empty before. And I think I'm falling in love with her.* "If you want to make love again, I'll try to think of some more reasons we should get married. There's probably one or two good excuses I haven't thought of yet, but—" He kissed her neck, burying deep into the curve, smelling her clean scent, wanting her already.

"Creed," she said, "I've been through one marriage. And my nieces have already been through marriages that didn't work out for their parents. Do you know what I mean?"

"I do, my doubting angel." He kissed her hand. "You want something solid for your nieces. You won't settle for anything less than a real family. And you think I'm your man. Hand me that bag on the nightstand, please."

"Not right now, Creed, this is serious." Aberdeen melted his heart with her big pleading eyes that melted his heart. She was such a delicate little thing. He wouldn't hurt her for the world. "I feel like you're playing with me."

"Oh, no. I wouldn't. Well, sometimes I will, in fact a lot of times I will, but not about a marriage agreement. I'm very serious about agreements. Hand me my bag, sugar."

She shook her head. "Creed, I can't make love when you've got me tied in knots. I couldn't think. I couldn't focus. I just don't understand why you want to marry—"

He gave her a tiny slap on the backside. "Aberdeen, will you please hand me that sack on the nightstand? Or do I have to get it myself?"

"Here's your silly old sack," she said, snatching it up and flinging it at him. "But I'm not saying yes, so don't even ask."

He raised a brow. "No yes?"

"No. Absolutely not." She looked fit to be tied, as if she'd love to kick him out of her bed.

Creed sighed. "Is that your final answer?"

"In fact, it is. No woman can make love when the man who is in her bed is being an absolute ass."

"Whoa, them's fighting words from a preacher." Creed grinned at her. "Just so I can get this straight," he said, reaching into the bag and pulling out a jeweler's box, which he opened, "you're saying no?"

She stared at the box he opened for her to view. It contained a heart-shaped diamond, which he was pretty proud of picking out this morning on his way for the condoms and granola bars.

"Creed," she said, sounding shocked and choked-up, and he snapped the box shut and put it back in the bag.

"Too bad," he said. "The jeweler promised me no woman could say no to this ring. He said a woman would have to have a heart of stone to refuse it. He said—"

"You're crazy! I knew it when I first met you. I know you're crazy, and I know better than to throw myself to the wind like this, but I'm going to ride this ride, cowboy, and I swear, if you turn out to be a weirdo, I'll be really ticked at you."

He kissed her, and she burst into tears, and threw her arms around his neck. "There, there," he said, "having a weirdo for a husband wouldn't be that bad, would it?"

"Creed, give me my ring," Aberdeen said, trying not to giggle against his neck as he held her.

"Greedy," he murmured, "but I don't mind." He took the ring from the box and slipped it on her finger, and for a moment, they both admired it in the light that spilled into the bedroom through the lace curtains.

"You are a weirdo," Aberdeen said, "and I don't know why I'm jumping off a cliff into alligator-infested waters."

Creed just grinned at her. "I'll let you get on top, future Mrs. Callahan, if you're sweet, and this time, you can ride me bareback."

Aberdeen looked at him, not sure if she trusted him or not, not sure exactly of what she wanted to feel for him. But Creed understood she'd been let down before, so he tugged her on top of him, and then smiled to himself when after a moment she said, "This time, I'm going to please you, cowboy."

Aunt Fiona was right, as usual. This marriage stuff is going to be a piece of cake. I feel like I'm winning again—finally.

Chapter Eleven

Marriage was *not* going to be a piece of cake. It was going to be as nerve-racking as any event he'd ever ridden in—only this time, he was pretty certain getting stomped by a bull was less traumatic than what he was experiencing now. Creed found himself waiting outside Aberdeen's family home, cooling his heels before the big intro. The girls were inside, getting reacquainted with their aunt and Johnny. Aberdeen wanted to introduce him to her family after she had a chance to go inside and prepare them for the big news.

He was nervous. And it was all because of the little girls. He'd thought they'd liked him for the brief moments they met him before—but what if they'd changed their minds? Kids did that. He knew from experience. He wasn't certain he would have wanted a new father when he was a kid. Maybe he wouldn't. He and his brothers probably would have given a new father a rough road—he was certain they would have. They'd given everybody a rough road on principle, except Fiona. She wouldn't have put up with that type of nonsense, and besides, she'd always been able to out-think them.

He was pretty certain the little girlies might be able to out-think him, too. Girls had mercurial brains, and at their tender ages, they probably had mercurial set on high.

He was sweating bullets.

He should have brought some teddy bears or something. Big pieces of candy. Cowgirl hats. Anything to break the ice and get the girls to see him in a positive light.

"Creed, come in." Aberdeen smiled out the door at him, and he told his restless heart to simmer down. It was going to be okay.

He stepped inside the small Montana house—and found himself on the receiving end of frowns from everyone in the family except Johnny.

"Good man," Johnny said, clapping him on the back, and Creed felt better.

"You might have warned me you were setting me up," Creed groused under his breath, and Johnny laughed.

"You struck me as the kind of man who didn't need a warning," Johnny said. "These are our parents. Mom, Dad, this is Creed Callahan."

He was definitely not getting the red carpet treatment. Mr. and Mrs. Donovan wore scowls the size of Texas. "Hello," he said, stepping forward to shake their hands, "it's a pleasure to meet you."

He got the fastest handshakes he'd ever had. No warmth there. Creed stepped back, telling himself he'd probably feel the same way if he had little girls and some cowboy was slinking around. The girls looked up at him shyly, their eyes huge, and Creed had to smile. He did have little girls now—three of them—and he was going to scowl when boys came knocking on his door for them.

"Well," Aberdeen said, "Creed, sit down, please. Make yourself comfortable."

"You're marrying my daughter," Mr. Donovan said, and Creed nodded.

"That's the plan, sir."

"I don't think I care for that plan."

Creed glanced at Johnny, surprised. Johnny shrugged at him.

"I'm sorry to hear that," Creed finally said, trying to sound respectable. "Your daughter will be in good hands, I promise."

"We know nothing about you," Mrs. Donovan said.

"Mom," Aberdeen said, "I'm marrying him. You can be nice, or you can both be annoying, but this man is my choice. So you'll just have to accept it."

"You're not taking the girls," Mrs. Donovan said, and Creed went tense.

"Yes, I am, as soon as I clear it with the judge." Aberdeen got to her feet, abandoning the pretense of a welcome-home party. Creed felt sorry for her. Aunt Fiona had kept them in line over the years, but she'd never been rude to them. He glanced at the tiny girls, and they stared back at him, not smiling.

His heart withered to the size of a gumdrop. He wanted them to like him so badly, and at the moment they just seemed confused.

"The judge won't approve it." Mr. Donovan seemed confident about that. "He feels they are better off here, near us."

"All right. Come on, Creed." Aberdeen swept to the door. Creed recognized his cue and followed dutifully, not understanding his role in the script but sensing his bride-to-be was working on a game plan.

Mrs. Donovan shot to her feet. "Where are you going?"

"Back to Wyoming," Aberdeen said, and Johnny followed her to the door. Johnny might have set him up, Creed realized, but he definitely had his sister's back.

"You can't just leave!" Mrs. Donovan exclaimed.

"I can. I will. And I am."

"Wait!" Mrs. Donovan sounded panicked. "What are we going to do with the girls?"

"Raise them," Aberdeen said, and Creed could see her lips were tight. She was angry, loaded for bear, and he didn't ever want to see her look at him like that. "Maybe you'll do a better job with them than you did with us."

"Hang on a minute," Mr. Donovan said. "Let's just all calm down."

"I'm past calm," Aberdeen said. "Calm isn't available to me at the moment."

The little girls started to cry. Creed's heart broke. "Oh," he murmured, not sure what to do, completely undone by the waterworks. "I think I'll wait outside," he said, and headed toward Johnny's truck. This was such bad karma that he was going to kiss Aunt Fiona as soon as he got back to Rancho Diablo. He'd never realized before how much her steadfast parenting had colored his existence happy. Of course, she was going to box his ears when she found out he was getting married and she didn't get to arrange it, and that made him feel a bit more resourceful.

He sat in the truck, feeling like a teenager. After a few moments, Mrs. Donovan came to his window. "Mr. Callahan," she said, her eyes bright. He thought she'd been crying.

"Yes, ma'am? Please call me Creed."

"Will you please come back inside and have a cup of tea before you depart?"

He looked at her, and she looked back at him with a sad expression, and he realized she was scared.

"You know," he said softly, "I'm not taking her away from you forever. And you will always be welcome at Rancho Diablo. We like having family around."

Tears jumped into her eyes. She nodded. "Tea?"

"I'd be honored," he said, and followed his future mother-in-law into the house.

"WHAT DID YOU say to her?" Aberdeen asked, watching her mother ply Creed with cupcakes and tea.

"I said I liked tea a whole lot."

Creed filled his plate up with sweets, and balanced Lincoln Rose on his knee as though he'd done it a thousand times before. Aberdeen was astonished. Good father material wasn't something she'd put on her checklist when she'd decided to seduce Creed. The shock of discovering that he might have potential in this area warmed her heart. The most important thing in the world to her right now was the welfare of her nieces—she'd do anything to protect their futures, make sure their lives were as comfortable and normal as possible under the circumstances.

Never had she suspected that Creed might be a truly willing participant in her goal. He sure looked like it now, with all her nieces standing close to him, eating him up with their eyes like they'd never seen a real man before. They'd had Johnny, but she and Johnny hadn't been around much, not knowing that Diane's marriage was in trouble. So Creed garnered a lot of attention from the girls. And he seemed to return that attention, with affection thrown in.

It's an agreement. We made an agreement. He's

merely keeping up his part of the bargain. I wanted stability, and he wanted stability, and neither of us ever said anything about permanent. Or love.

So don't do it. Don't go falling in love when you know that's not a realistic ending to the story. Wild never settles down forever—and he never said forever anyway.

"More tea?" she said to Creed, and he smiled at her, his gaze kind and patient as he held the girls, and she felt heat run all over her. And another chip fell off her heart.

"TO BE HONEST," Johnny said to Creed when they'd gone outside to throw a ball for the little nieces, "I didn't mean for you to propose to my sister."

Creed looked at him, then back at the porch where Aberdeen was standing with her parents, watching the game. The small house framed them. If he hadn't known better, he would have thought this was a happy family. However, it wasn't anything he wasn't experienced with, so Creed felt pretty comfortable. "What did you have in mind, then?"

"I thought it would be a good idea to give Aberdeen something new to look at. Re-ride was old, you were new." Johnny grinned. "I wanted her to know that there were other fish in the sea."

"I'm sure there've been plenty of fish swimming her way," Creed said, his tone mild.

"Yeah, but she's not much for catching them." Johnny tossed the ball, and the pink toy bounced toward the girls who squealed and tried to catch it with uncoordinated hands. "Anyway, I just wanted you to know that you're taking on a pretty tall order with us."

"Tall doesn't bother me." Creed looked at the girls, then glanced back at Aberdeen. Her hair shone in the

Montana sunlight and she was smiling at him. "However, you'll have to come to New Mexico to see her, my friend, so I hope you thought through your plan in its entirety."

"That's the way it is, huh?"

"That's the way it is." Creed nodded. "We've got plenty of space for you, too, if you're of a mind to see a different topography."

Johnny grinned. "I hear New Mexico is nice this time of year."

Creed nodded, but his gaze was on Aberdeen again, and all he could think about was that New Mexico was going to be really nice, better than nice, when he had his little preacher lady sleeping in his big bed. Naked. Naked, warm and willing.

She waved at him, and he smiled, feeling like the big bad wolf. The happiest wolf in the canyons.

AFTER HE'D CHARMED Aberdeen's folks—who warmed to him quickly after their initial resistance—and after he'd cleared hurdles with the judge, Creed placed one last phone call to warn his family of their impending change in lifestyle.

"Hello," Rafe said, and Creed grinned.

"Hello, yourself. If you've got the time, we need a ride."

His twin sighed. "I'm not flying up there just to pick up your lazy butt."

Creed had taken himself out to the small backyard after dinner to have this conversation. Johnny and Aberdeen were tucking the little girls into bed, so he had time to sound the alarm. "You'll be picking up my lazy butt and a few very busy little bottoms."

"Well, now, that sounds more interesting. How are these bottoms? Female, I hope?"

Creed grinned. "Very much so."

"Round and cute?"

"The cutest, roundest tushes you ever saw."

"So I should shave."

"Definitely. You'll regret it if you don't. You don't want to scare them." Creed thought about the small dolls that would be traveling with him and held back a laugh.

"You flying your own entertainment in for Fiona's charity ball?"

"You might say I am."

"Well, consider me your eager pilot. Where and what time do you need a pick-up?"

One of the benefits of having an ex-military pilot who'd spent time flying for private corporations was that the family had their own plane. Rafe was an excellent pilot, and letting him fly them home would be easier on the girls. Creed hadn't yet told Aberdeen, but he was looking forward to surprising her. "Tomorrow, in Spring, Montana. Plan on me, a friend and four damsels, you might say."

Rafe whistled. "You *have* been busy."

"Be on your best behavior. And ask Aunt Fiona to get the guest house ready for visitors, will you?"

"She's going to be thrilled that you're falling into line." Rafe laughed. "I should have known that all this talk of watching over a bar for some guy was just a ruse."

"Probably you should have."

"I don't know if Fiona's going to be cool with you sleeping in the guest house with a bunch of women. On the other hand she's not totally uptight, and she is hoping to marry you off," Rafe mused. "She did say she thought you were the least likely of all of us to ever settle down. So she'll probably be okay with it."

"My ladies are pretty fine. Aunt Fiona will be all right after the initial shock."

"Bombshells, huh? Are you sharing?"

"You can hold them any time you like. Except for my particular favorite, of course. Oh, and bring your headset. They can be loud. Girl chatter and all that. Wild times."

"You old dog," Rafe said, his tone admiring. "And everyone says you're the slow twin. Boy, did you have everybody fooled."

"See you tomorrow," Creed said, and turned off his phone. He went to find Aberdeen, who was sitting in the family room alone. She appeared slightly anxious as her gaze settled on him. "Hello."

"Hi." She smiled, but he thought she looked ner-vous. "Girls asleep?"

"Johnny's reading to them. Lincoln Rose is asleep, the other two are excited about the trip tomorrow."

Creed nodded, sitting next to her on the sofa. "I hope you don't mind flying."

Aberdeen looked at him. "We're flying to New Mexico?"

"It'll be easier on the girls than a few days' drive."

"Thank you." Aberdeen smiled. "That's considerate of you, Creed."

"It is. I plan to get my reward after we're married."

Aberdeen's eyes widened. "After?"

"Well, yes. You'll have to wait to have me until you've made an honest man of me." He was pretty proud of his plan. He knew she had probably been thinking of how everything was going to work out between them. Sooner or later, she'd get worried about the silly stuff. Like, she wouldn't want to sleep with him at his ranch until they were married; it wouldn't be decent. She was, after all, a minister. She would worry about such things. She was also a new mother to children. She would be concerned about propriety. He intended to take all those worries right out of her busy little mind.

"I think you are an honest man," Aberdeen said shyly.

"Well, aren't you just a little angel cake," he said, pleased, and dropped a kiss on her nose. "But you're still not having me until you put the ring on my finger."

Aberdeen laughed. "You're horrible."

"But you like it." He put her head against his shoulder, enjoying holding her in the quiet family room.

"I'm so glad you weren't bothered by my folks," Aberdeen said softly. "They can be busybodies."

"Oh, I know all about well-meaning interference. I'm an experienced hand. I just hope you know what you're getting yourself into, little lady."

She smiled and leaned closer, and Creed closed his eyes, contented. Of course she had no idea what she was stepping into. He wasn't certain what was waiting back home for them, either. All he did know was that he'd told her she had to wait until they were married to have him again.

But they hadn't set a wedding date.

He felt like he was holding his breath—and he needed to breathe again. Soon.

Chapter Twelve

When Rafe met them at the plane, he was in full wolf mode. Dark aviator glasses, new jeans, dark Western shirt, dress boots. Even a sterling bolo with a turquoise stone. The kind of lone wolf any woman would lick her chops over.

Only Creed's ladies didn't really have chops yet, just gums. "Here you go," he told Rafe, and handed him the baby. "This is Lincoln Rose. Lincoln, don't be scared of ugly, honey. He tries hard but he's just not handsome like me."

Lincoln Rose stared at Rafe. Rafe stared back at her, just as bemused. Creed grinned and went to walk the next little girl up the stairs. "This is my brother, honey. You can call him Uncle Rafe if you want to, Ashley," Creed said, even though she didn't talk much yet. "Let's figure out how to strap your car seat in, okay? This plane has never seen a baby seat. But I'm pretty sure we can figure it out." He put her favorite stuffed animal and a small book beside her, then went back to the front of the plane. "And I see you've met my last little girl." Creed grinned at his brother, who still held Lincoln Rose as he latched eyes on Aberdeen with appreciation. "And this is the lady I mentioned was my special girl. Aberdeen, this is my brother, Rafe. Rafe, this is my fiancée, Aberdeen Donovan, and this little munchkin is Suzanne. Her sisters call her Suzu. And bringing up the rear is our nanny, Johnny Donovan."

"You look just like Creed," Aberdeen said. "Creed, you didn't tell me you had a twin."

"No reason to reveal all the sordid details." Creed waved Johnny toward the back and took Lincoln Rose from his brother.

"Details like how you travel in style?" Johnny said. "This is a sweet ride."

"Well, it helps to get around the country fast. We do a lot of deals here and there." Creed looked at Aberdeen. "Do you want to be co-pilot, honey?"

"No," Aberdeen said, "Thank you. I'll just sit back and try to decide how I got myself into this."

Creed grinned. "Make yourself comfortable. I'm going to help Rafe fly this rust bucket. Are we good to go, pilot?"

Rafe still seemed stunned as he looked over his new cargo of toys and babies. "Three little girls," he said, his tone amazed. "Are you trying to beat Pete?" he asked, and Creed glared at him.

"Do you see a fourth?" Creed asked.

"Who's Pete?" Aberdeen asked.

"Our brother who was first to the altar, and first to hit the baby lotto," Rafe said cheerfully.

"What were you supposed to beat him at, Creed?" Aberdeen asked.

Rafe glanced at Creed, who wished his brother had laryngitis. "I'm not trying to beat anybody at anything," Creed said. "Don't you worry your pretty little head about anything my numbskull of a brother says."

Rafe nodded. "That's right. Ignore me. I'm a pig at times."

"Most of the time. Let's fly." Creed dragged his brother into the cockpit.

"She doesn't know, does she?" Rafe asked as they settled in.

"I saw no reason to mention the baby-making aspects of Fiona's plan. It had no bearing on my decision."

"You sure?" Rafe asked.

"More than sure. Otherwise, there would be a fourth."

"And there's not?"

"Do you see a fourth?" Creed glared at Rafe again.

"I'm just wondering," Rafe said. "As your twin, it's my duty to wonder."

"Skip your duty, okay?"

Rafe switched on some controls. "I should have known that when you said you were keeping an eye on a bar, you meant a nursery."

"No, I meant a bar. I didn't have plans to get engaged when I left."

"So you found yourself in a bar and then a bed." Rafe sounded tickled. "And there were three bonuses, and so you realized this was a primo opportunity to get out of Fiona's line of fire. And maybe even beat Pete."

"No," Creed said, "because there's nothing to beat Pete for. We have no ranch, per se. Therefore, no need to have children by the dozen."

"Oh. You hadn't heard. You've been gone." Rafe slowly taxied on to the runway. "We're all supposed to settle down, if we want to, to try to keep Bode from getting the ranch."

"It's no guarantee."

"But you don't know that Fiona says that competition

head at Creed. "You told Rafe you were bringing bomb-shells, you ruffian."

"I couldn't resist, Aunt Fiona." Creed grinned, clearly proud of himself.

"These are the prettiest bombshells I've ever seen," Fiona said. "I'll have to send out for some cribs, though. And anything else you require, Aberdeen. We don't have enough children at Rancho Diablo, so we'll be happy to gear up for these. You'll just have to let us know what babies need. My nephews have been a wee bit on the slow side about starting families." She sent Creed a teasing smile. "Is there anything else you'd like to spring on us, Creed?"

"Introductions first, Aunt Fiona." He went through the litany of brothers, and Aberdeen felt nearly over-whelmed by all the big men around her. Johnny seemed right at home. But then, another woman came forward, pushing a big-wheeled pram over the driveway, and Su-zanne and Ashley went over to see what was inside.

"Babies," Ashley said, and Creed laughed.

"This is Pete's wife, Jackie. Jackie, this is Aberdeen Donovan."

Jackie smiled at her; Aberdeen felt that she'd found a friend.

"We'll have a lot to talk about," Jackie said.

"Yes, we will," Fiona said. "Come inside and let's have tea. I'm sure you're starving, Aberdeen." She took Lincoln Rose in her arms and headed toward the house. Aberdeen and Jackie followed.

"I'm starving, too," Creed said, watching the ladies walk away.

Sam laughed. "Not for love."

Jonas shook his head. "Did you buy that big diamond she's wearing?"

Creed shrugged. "It isn't that big."

"You're getting married?" Judah asked. "You were only gone a few days!"

"It feels right," Creed said, grinning at them.

"You're trying to win," Pete said. "You're trying to beat me."

Creed clapped his brother on the back. "Nope. I'd have to go for four to win, and I'm pretty good at knowing my limits, bro. The gold medal is all yours."

Pete grinned. "I hope you warned Aberdeen."

"About what?" Creed scowled as he and his brothers and Johnny walked toward the house, each carrying a suitcase. Burke tried to help carry one, but the brothers told him diaper bags were their responsibility, and Burke gladly went to park the van instead.

"About the bet. Which is a really dumb bet, if you ask me," Pete said. "I wasn't even trying, and look what happened to me. I just wanted to get married."

"It's almost like you got hit by a magic spell," Sam mused. "Who would have ever thought you could father three adorable little girls?"

"I don't know what to say about that," Pete groused. "I think it was more like a miracle. But besides that, I'm more than capable of fathering adorable, thanks. You'll be the one who has ugly."

"There's no such thing as an ugly baby." Jonas opened the door. "Have you ever seen an ugly baby? They don't exist. I'm a doctor, I know."

"You're a heart specialist, don't overreach your specialty." Creed shook his head. "But no, we're not going to bring up the baby bet, and we're not going to talk about ranch problems or anything like that. I'm trying to get the woman to marry me, not leave in a dust cloud." It could happen. Aberdeen could get cold feet. She had that cold-feet look about her right now. Creed knew she was still annoyed about Rafe's conversation with him in the plane. He also knew she'd been a bit rattled by the size of Rancho Diablo. Or maybe by its faraway location. Whatever it was, he needed time to iron it out of her without his brothers bringing up Callahan drama. "So just pull your hats down over your mouths if you have to," he told his brothers, "and let's not talk about anything we have going on that's *unusual*."

"Oh, he likes this one," Sam whispered to his brothers.

"You're talking about my sister like I'm not here," Johnny said.

"Sorry," Sam said. "You look like one of us. You could be a Callahan. We can be easily confused." He grinned. "We separate ourselves into the bachelors and the down-for-the-count."

"I'm not down—oh, never mind." Creed shook his head. "Johnny, don't listen to anything we say. We mean well. Some of us just blab too much."

Johnny shrugged. "I hear it all the time in the bar. Yak, yak, yak."

Jonas jerked his head toward the barn. "While the ladies chat, let us show you the set-up."

Creed hung back as his brothers headed out. He was pretty certain that if he was smart—and he thought he was where women were concerned—he'd better hang around and try to iron some of the kinks out of his little woman. She had a mulish look in her eyes whenever he caught her gaze, and he knew too well that mulish females were not receptive to men. He sat down by Aberdeen and pulled Lincoln Rose into his lap. "Take you for a buggy ride around the property when you've had a chance to rest?"

Aberdeen looked at him. "Is it story time?"

"I think so." Creed nodded. "Better late than never, huh?"

"We'll babysit," Jackie said, and Fiona nodded eagerly.

"And it's romantic on the ranch at night," Jackie said. "Trust me, Aberdeen, you want to take a spin on the ranch."

Aberdeen looked at Creed, and he smiled, and though she didn't smile back at him, he thought, she wasn't beaning him with a baby bottle, either—and that was the best sign he had at the moment.

"Romance," he said so only she could hear, "are you up for that?"

"We'll see how good your story is," she said, and Creed sank back in the sofa, looking at Lincoln Rose.

"Any tips on good stories?" he asked the baby, but she just looked at him. "I don't know any, either," he said, and Fiona said, "Then I suggest you get it in gear, nephew. Once upon a time, cowboy poets lived by their ability to tell stories. Live the legend."

Aberdeen raised a brow at him, and he decided right then and there that whatever she wanted, the lady was going to get.

Chapter Thirteen

Aberdeen could tell Creed was dying to get her alone. She wasn't entirely reluctant. Story time didn't sound horrible—and in spite of the conversation she'd overheard between Creed and his twin, she was willing to give him a chance to explain.

And to kiss her breathless.

Burke entered the room with a tall, distinguished-looking guest, and the room went silent.

"Well, Bode Jenkins," Fiona said, rising to her feet. "To what do we owe this unpleasant occurrence?"

Bode smiled at her thinly, then glanced at Aberdeen's daughters. "A little bird told me that you were welcoming visitors. You know how I hate not being invited to a party, Fiona." He sent a welcoming smile to Aberdeen, but instead of feeling welcomed, her skin chilled.

Creed stood, and Jonas stood with him. Sam followed, as did Rafe, Pete and Judah. Aberdeen glanced at Creed, whose face seemed suddenly set in granite. The brothers looked ready for an old-style Western shoot-out, which bewildered her.

"Now, Bode," Fiona said, "you have no business being here."

"You should be neighborly, Fiona," Bode said, his

tone silky. "When Sabrina told me you were expecting visitors, I just had to come and see what good things were happening around my future ranch. One day," he ruminated, "I'm going to cover this place over with concrete to build the biggest tourist center you ever dreamed of."

The brothers folded their arms, standing silent. If this man's visit was about her arrival, then Aberdeen wanted no part of it. She grabbed Lincoln Rose and held her in her lap, either for comfort or to protect her from what felt like an oncoming storm, she wasn't certain. Her sisters naturally followed Lincoln Rose, hugging to Aberdeen's side for protection.

But then Ashley broke away and went to Creed, who picked her up in his big, strong arms. Bode smiled, his mouth barely more than a grimace. "Looks like you're growing quite the family, Fiona," he said, glancing at Pete's and Jackie's three daughters. "Another birdie told me that you're paying your sons to get wives and have babies so you can make the claim that Rancho Diablo has its own population and therefore shouldn't be subject to the laws of the nation. It won't work, Fiona, if that's what's on your mind."

"Never mind what's on her mind," Creed said, his voice a growl. "If you've stated your business, Jenkins, go."

Bode looked at Aberdeen. Her skin jumped into a crawling shiver. She clutched her two nieces to her. "I'm not going without giving my gift to the new bride-to-be," he murmured, his gaze alight with what looked like unholy fire to Aberdeen. "Will you walk outside with me, my dear?"

"I'm sorry that I can't," Aberdeen said. "My nieces

wouldn't like me leaving them. We've just gotten in from a long day of traveling. I'm sure you'll understand."

Creed shot her a look of approval.

"That's too bad," Bode said. "There's someone I want you to meet."

"Is Sabrina outside?" Fiona frowned. "Why don't you bring her in?"

"Sabrina says she thinks she's coming down with a cold. She didn't want to give it to anyone." Bode shrugged. "I've just learned Sabrina is a fortune-teller. I wanted her to tell your fortune as a gift, Miss—"

"Donovan," Aberdeen said. "I don't believe in fortune-telling, Mr. Jenkins. Please tell your friend I'll be happy to meet her at another time when she isn't under the weather."

But then she realized that Fiona was staring at Bode, her brows pinched and low. Aberdeen sank back into her chair, glancing at Creed, who watched Bode like a hawk.

"Sabrina is a home-care provider," Fiona said, "who happens to have a gift. Why do you sound so irregular about it, Bode?"

He smiled at Fiona, but it wasn't a friendly smile. "I think you've tried to set me up, Fiona Callahan. And I don't take kindly to trickery."

"I don't know what you're talking about," Fiona snapped. "Don't be obtuse."

"Then let me be clear. You hired Sabrina McKinley to spy on me."

"Nonsense," Fiona shot back. "Why would I do that?"

"You'll do anything you can to save your ranch." Bode tapped his walking stick with impatience. "My daughter Julie figured it all out," he said. "She learned from one of your sons that Sabrina had been here one night."

"So?" Fiona said, her tone rich with contempt.

"So it was an easy feat for Julie to run a background check on Sabrina. Turns out she was traveling with some kind of circus."

"Is that a crime?" Jonas asked. "Last I knew, a circus was a place for hard-working people to have a job with some travel and do what they like to do."

"I'd be careful if I was you, Jonas," Bode said, his tone measured, "your little aunt can get in a lot of trouble for helping someone forge documents of employment and employment history."

Creed snorted. "How would Aunt Fiona do that?"

"Why don't you tell them, Fiona?" Bode stepped closer to Aberdeen, gazing down at the little girls she held. "I'd be cognizant, my dear, were I you, that this family loves games. And not games of the puzzle and Scrabble variety. Games where they use you as a pawn. You'll figure out soon enough what your role is, but only you can decide if you want to be a piece that's played."

"How dare you?" Aberdeen snapped. "Sir, I'll have you know that I'm a minister. I've met people from all walks of life, heard their stories, ached with their troubles, celebrated their joy. You know nothing about me at all, so don't assume I don't know how to take care of myself and those I love."

"I only wish to give you the gift of knowledge," Bode replied.

Aberdeen shook her head. "Gift unaccepted and unneeded. Creed, I'd like to take the girls to their room now." She stood, and Burke materialized at her side.

"I'll take Miss Donovan to her room," Burke said. "The golf cart should carry everyone nicely."

"I'm going out to see Sabrina," Jonas said, and Bode said, "She's not up to seeing—"

"She'll see me," Jonas snapped.

Judah trailed after Jonas. "I'm not being a bodyguard or anything," he told Bode as he walked by him, "I'm just damn nosy."

The two men left. Creed handed Lincoln Rose to Burke. Fiona stood, looking like a queen of a castle.

"You've caused enough of an uproar for one night, Bode. Out you go."

"We're at war, Fiona," Bode said, and she said, "Damn right we are."

"That's enough," Creed said. "If you don't go, Jenkins, we'll throw your worthless hide out."

Aberdeen followed Burke outside, with a last glance back at Creed. He'd stepped close to Bode, protectively standing between his aunt and the enemy, and Aberdeen realized that Creed was a man who guarded his own. He looked fierce, dangerous, nothing at all like the man who romanced her and seduced her until she wanted to do whatever it took to make him happy.

Yet, looking back at Creed, Aberdeen also realized she had no idea what was going on in this family. It was as if she'd landed in a strange new world, and the man she'd agreed to marry had suddenly turned into a surly lion.

Johnny took one of the girls in his arms, following her out, and as their eyes met, she knew her brother was re-thinking her cowboy fiancé, too.

"BUSTED," SAM SAID, and Creed nodded. Bode had left,

his demeanor pleased. Whatever he'd come to do, he felt he'd succeeded.

"I think you are busted, Aunt," Creed said. "He knows all about your plan. I don't think Sabrina would have ratted you out unless he threatened her."

"Oh, pooh." Fiona waved a hand. "Bode is my puppet. He jumps when I pull his strings."

Creed crooked a brow at his aunt. "You told Sabrina to enlighten him with the fortune-teller gag?"

"Seemed simpler than having him fish around and find out she's actually an investigative reporter." Fiona shrugged, looking pleased with herself. "Now he thinks he knows something he probably won't go digging around in her background. At the moment, he thinks he stole her from me, so he's pleased. It's not that hard to do a search on the computer for people these days, you know."

Creed shook his head. "You deal with her," he told his brothers. "I have a fiancée and three little ladies to settle in to the guest house."

His brothers looked as though they wished he would keep on with the line of questioning he'd been peppering their cagey aunt with, but he had promised romance to a pretty parson, and he was going to do just that.

CREED WALKED INTO the guest house right after Aberdeen had finished tidying the girls up and putting them in their jammies. The girls were tired, too exhausted for a bedtime story, so Aberdeen kissed them and put them in their little beds with rails—except for Lincoln Rose, who had her own lovely white crib. "Your aunt is amazing," she told Creed, who nodded.

"She amazes everyone."

"She's thought of everything." Aberdeen pointed around the room, showing the toys and extra diapers and even a tray of snacks and drinks on a wrought-iron tray on the dresser. "How did she do all this so quickly?"

"A lot of this is Burke's doing," Creed said, "but Fiona is the best. We were spoiled growing up."

"I could guess that." Aberdeen looked around the room. "It's clear that she spent a lot of time thinking about what children need to be comfortable."

Creed frowned. Aunt Fiona hadn't known about the girls. He hadn't told anyone, not even Rafe. He'd wanted them to get to know Aberdeen and the girls on their own, and not from anything he mentioned on a phone call.

Somehow Aunt Fiona had figured him out. He sighed. "No moss grows under her feet."

"Well, I'm very grateful. And now, if you don't mind, I'm going to bed." She turned her back on Creed, letting him know that he need not expect a goodnight kiss. She wasn't ready to go into all the details of everything he was keeping from her, but at this moment she was bone-tired. And her nieces would be up early, no doubt. Tomorrow she'd make Creed tell her what was going on with the scary neighbor and Rancho Diablo.

At least those were her plans, until she felt Creed standing behind her, his body close and warm against her back. She closed her eyes, drinking in his nearness and his strength. He ran his hands down the length of her arms, winding her fingers into his, and Aberdeen's resistance slowly ebbed away.

He dropped a kiss on the back of her neck, sending a delightful shiver over her.

"I'm sorry about tonight," he murmured against her skin. "I had romantic plans for us."

"It may be hard to find time for romance with all the commotion you have going on here. I thought my family tree was thick with drama."

He turned her toward him, his dark gaze searching hers. "I know you're wondering about a lot of things. I'll tell you a few family yarns in between riding lessons with the girls."

"Not my girls," Aberdeen said, her heart jumping.

"No time like the present for them to get in the saddle." Creed winked at her. "And you, too. You'll make a wonderful cowgirl."

"Sorry, no." Aberdeen laughed. "Lincoln Rose is staying right in her comfy stroller. My other two nieces can look at the horses, but there'll be no saddle-training for them."

"We'll see," Creed said, his tone purposefully mysterious. "Learning to ride a horse is just like learning how to swim."

"Will not happen," she reiterated, and stepped away from his warmth. She already wanted to fall into his arms, and after everything she'd heard today, she'd be absolutely out of her head to do such a thing. If she'd ever thought Creed was wild, she had only to come here to find out that he probably was—at the very minimum, he lived by his own code. And the judge was looking for stability in her life before he awarded her permanent custody of her nieces. An adoption application needed to be smooth as well. She shot Creed a glance over her shoulder, checking him out, noting that his gaze never left her. He was protective, he was kind, he was strong. She was falling in love with him—had fallen in love with him—but there were little people to consider. Her own heart needed to be more cautious, not tripping into love just because the man could romance her beyond her wildest imaginings. "Goodnight, Creed," she said, and after a moment, he nodded.

"Sweet dreams," he said, and then before she could steel herself against him, he kissed her, pinning his fingers into her waist, pulling her against him.

And then he left, probably fully aware that he'd just set her blood to boil. Tired as she was, she was going to be thinking about him for a long time, well past her bedtime—the rogue. And she was absolutely wild for him.

She wished Creed was sleeping in her bed tonight.

Chapter Fourteen

"You can't marry her," Aunt Fiona said when Creed went back to the main house. Fiona was sitting in the library in front of a window, staring out into the darkness. Burke had placed a coffee cup and a plate of cookies on the table. Creed recognized the signs of a family powwow, so he took the chair opposite Fiona and said, "I'm surprised you'd say that, Aunt. Doesn't Aberdeen fill the bill?"

Fiona gave him a sideways glance. "If there was a bill to be filled, I'm sure she'd do quite well. However, I don't believe in doing things in half measures, and I think that's what you're doing, Creed."

He nodded at the cup Burke placed beside him, and sipped gratefully. He didn't need caffeine to keep up with Fiona, but he did need fortification. It was going to be a stirring debate. "You're talking about the little girls."

Fiona shrugged. "They're darling. They deserve your best. We don't have a best to give them at the moment, as Bode's untimely visit indicates."

"We'll be fine. Give me the real reason you're protesting against me marrying her."

"Stability. We don't have that." Fiona sighed. "Have you told Aberdeen about this situation?"

"No. It didn't seem necessary. I'll take care of her and the children."

Fiona nodded. "I would expect that. However, we're at war here. Bode was sizing us up. I don't mind saying I'm afraid."

Creed shrugged. "I'm not afraid of that old man."

"You should be. He intends to make trouble."

"What's the worst he can do?"

Fiona looked at him. "You should know."

"I think the choice should be Aberdeen's."

Fiona nodded. "I agree. Be honest with her. Let her know that we're not the safe haven we may appear to be at first glance."

Creed didn't like that. He wanted to be able to give Aberdeen and the girls the comfort and safety he felt they needed. Protecting them was something his heart greatly desired. And yet, he knew Aunt Fiona's words of caution probably warranted consideration. "I'll think about it."

"Do you love her, Creed?" Fiona asked, her eyes searching his.

"Aberdeen is a good woman." He chose his words carefully, not really certain why he felt he had to hold back. "I think we complement each other."

After a moment, Fiona sat back in her chair. "Of course, you know that it's my fondest wish for you boys to be settled. I haven't hidden my desire to see you with families. But I wouldn't want to bring harm to anyone, Creed."

He stared at his aunt. Harm? He had no intention of causing Aberdeen any pain. Far from it. All her wanted to give her was joy. He wanted to take care of her. That's what they'd agreed upon between themselves: Each of them needed something from the other. He intended to keep his side of the bargain.

But as he looked at his little aunt fretting with her napkin and then turning to stare out the window, searching Rancho Diablo in the darkness, he realized she really was worried.

For the thousandth time in his life, he wished Bode Jenkins would somehow just fade out of their lives. But he knew that wasn't going to happen. They just couldn't be that lucky.

"If I only believed in fairy tales," Fiona murmured. "But I have to be practical."

"You pitting us against each other for the ranch is very practical." Creed smiled. "Nobody is complaining, are they?"

Fiona gave him a sharp look. "Is the ranch why you're marrying her?"

Creed drew in a deep breath. Why was he marrying Aberdeen—really? Was he using the ranch as an excuse to bolster his courage to give up bull riding, give up his unsettled ways and get connected to a future? Aberdeen, a ball and chain; the little girls, tiny shackles.

Actually, Creed thought, he was pretty sure the little girls were buoys, if anything, and Aberdeen, a life preserver. Before he'd met them, he'd been drowning in a sea of purposelessness. "I can't speak to my exact motivation for marrying Aberdeen Donovan," Creed said. "I haven't had time to pinpoint the reason. It could be gratitude, because I think she saved my life in the literal sense. It could be she appeals to the knight in me who feels a need to save a damsel in distress. It might even be that she's gotten under my skin and I just have to conquer that." Creed brightened. "Whatever it is, I like it, though."

Fiona smiled. "You do seem happy."

He grunted. "I haven't got it all figured out yet. But when I do, I'll let you know."

TWO WEEKS LATER, the magic still hadn't worn off. Mornings bloomed so pretty and sunny that Aberdeen found herself awestruck by the beauty of the New Mexico landscape. Riding in the golf cart with Burke, who'd come to get her and the girls for breakfast, Aberdeen couldn't imagine anything more beautiful than Rancho Diablo on a summer morning.

And the girls seemed tranquil, curious about their surroundings, staring with wide eyes. Horses moved in a wooden corral, eager to watch the humans coming and going. Occasionally she saw a Callahan brother walking by, heading to work—they always turned to wave at the golf cart. She couldn't tell which brother was which yet, but the fact that Creed has such a large family was certainly comforting. She liked his family; she liked the affection they seemed to have for each other.

She was a little surprised that Creed was a twin, and that his brother, Pete, had triplets. What if she had a baby with Creed? What were the odds of having a multiple birth in a family that seemed to have them in the gene pool? The thought intimidated her, and even gave her a little insight into why Diane might have become overwhelmed. *One at a time would be best for me. I'd have four children to guide and grow and teach to walk the right path. I wonder if I'll be a good mother?*

When Aberdeen realized she was actually daydreaming about having Creed's baby, she forced herself to stop.

She was jumping light years ahead of what she needed to be thinking about, which was the girls and putting their needs first. They were so happy and so sweet, and she needed to do her best by them. She saw Johnny ride past in one of the trucks with a Callahan brother, and they waved at her and the girls, who got all excited when they saw their uncle. Johnny, it seemed, was fitting right in. He hadn't come in to the guest house last night, and she suspected he'd slept in the bunkhouse with the brothers. "Your uncle thinks he's going cowboy," she murmured to the girls, who ignored her in favor of staring at the horses and the occasional steer. It was good for Johnny to have this time to vacation a little. He'd had her back for so long he hadn't had much time to hang out, she realized. They'd both been tied to the bar, determined to make a success of it, buy that ticket out of Spring, Montana.

She hugged the girls to her. "Isn't this fun?"

They looked at her, their big eyes eager and excited. For the first time she felt herself relax, and when she saw Fiona come to the door, waving a dish towel at them in greeting, a smile lit her face. It was going to be all right, Aberdeen told herself. This was just a vacation for all of them, one that they needed. If it didn't work out between her and Creed, it would be fine—she and Johnny and the girls could go back home, create a life for themselves as if nothing special, nothing amazing, had happened.

As if she'd never fallen in love with Creed Callahan.

She took a deep breath as Burke stopped the golf cart in front of the mansion. Aberdeen got out, then she and Burke each helped the girls to the ground. Aberdeen turned to greet Fiona.

"Look who's here!" Fiona exclaimed, and Aberdeen halted in her tracks.

"Mommy!" Ashley cried, as she and Suzanne toddled off to greet Diane. Aberdeen's heart went still at the sight of her older sister, who did not look quite like the Diane she remembered. Cold water seemed to hit her in the face.

"Aberdeen!" Diane came to greet Aberdeen as if no time had passed, as if she hadn't abandoned her children. She threw her arms around Aberdeen, and Aberdeen found herself melting. She loved Diane with all her heart. Had she come to get her daughters? Aberdeen hoped so. A whole family would be the best thing for everyone.

"How are you doing?" Aberdeen asked her sister, leaning back to look at her, and Diane shook her head.

"We'll talk later. Right now, your wonderful mother-in-law-to-be has welcomed me into the fold," Diane said, and Aberdeen remembered that they had an audience.

"Yes. Aunt Fiona, this is my older sister, Diane." Aberdeen followed her nieces, who were trying to get up the steps to Fiona. Aberdeen carried Lincoln Rose, who didn't reach for her mother. The minute she saw Fiona, she reached for her, though. Fiona took her gladly, and Aberdeen and Diane shared a glance.

"I'm good with children," Fiona said, blushing a little that Diane's own daughter seemed to prefer her. "It's the granny syndrome."

"It's all right," Diane said quickly. "Come on, girls. Let's not leave Mrs. Callahan waiting."

"Oh." Fiona glanced back as they walked through the entryway. "Please, just call me Fiona. I've never been Mrs. Callahan."

"This is gorgeous," Diane whispered to Aberdeen. "How did you hook such a hot, rich hunk?"

"I haven't hooked him," Aberdeen said, hoping Fiona hadn't heard Diane.

"Well, find a way to do it. Listen to big sister. These are sweet digs."

"Diane," Aberdeen said, "what are you doing here? And how did you get here?"

"Mom and Dad told me where you were, and it's not that difficult to buy a plane ticket, Aberdeen."

"What about the French guy?"

"We'll talk later," Diane said as Fiona showed them in to a huge, country-style kitchen. At the long table, the largest Aberdeen had ever seen, settings were laid, and each place had a placard with their names in gold scrolling letters. There were even two high chairs for the youngest girls, with their own cards in scrolled letters. Each of the children had a stuffed toy beside her plate, and so they were eager to sit down, their eyes fastened on the stuffed horses.

"I hope you don't mind," Fiona said. "We have a gift shop in town and the owner is a friend of mine. I couldn't resist calling her up to get a few little things for the girls."

"Thank you so much," Diane said, and Aberdeen swallowed hard.

"Yes, thank you, Fiona. Girls, can you say thank you?"

The older ones did, and Lincoln Rose saw that her sisters were holding their horses so she reached for hers, too. And then Burke brought them breakfast, and Aberdeen tried to eat, even though her appetite was shot.

They were being treated like princesses—but the

thing was, she wasn't princess material. She eyed her sister surreptitiously; Diane seemed delighted by all the attention Fiona was showering on them, and Aberdeen felt like someone dropped into a storybook with a plot she hadn't yet caught up on.

"Quit looking so scared," Diane said under her breath. "Enjoy what the nice lady is trying to do for you. This is great." And she dug into the perfectly plated eggs and fruit as though she hadn't a care in the world.

"Diane," Aberdeen said quietly, so Fiona couldn't hear, even though she had her head in the fridge looking for something—a jam or jelly, she'd mentioned. "What are you doing here? Really?"

Diane smiled. "Little sister, I'm here to see my daughters. Who will soon be your daughters, by the looks of things."

"I think you should reconsider," Aberdeen said, desperation hatching inside her. "If you're not traveling with that guy, and you seem so happy now, I mean, don't you think…" She looked at her sister. "These are your children, Diane. You can't just abandon them."

"I'm not abandoning them." Diane took a bite of toast. "I simply recognize I'm not cut out to be a mother. I wish it were different, but it's not. I get depressed around them, Aberdeen. I know they're darling, and they seem so sweet and so cute, but when I'm alone with them, all I am is desperate. I'm not happy. I think I was trying to live a dream, but when my third husband left, I realized the dream had never been real." She looked at Aberdeen. "Please don't make me feel more guilty than I do already. It's not the best feeling in the world when a woman realizes she's a lousy mother. And, you know, we had a fairly dismal upbringing. I just don't want to do that to my own children."

Fiona came over to the table, setting down a bowl full of homemade strawberry jam. "I'm pretty proud of this," she said. "I had strawberries and blackberries shipped in special, and I redid my jam stock after I lost all of last year's." She beamed. "Tell me what you think of my blue-ribbon jam!"

Aberdeen tore her gaze away from her sister, numb, worried, and not in the mood for anything sweet. She glanced around at her nieces who seemed so amazed by all the treats and their stuffed horses that all they could do was sit very quietly, on their best behavior. They were obviously happy to see Diane, but not clingy, the way kids who hadn't seen their mother in a while would be. Aberdeen sighed and bit into a piece of jam-slathered toast. It was sweet and rich with berry taste. Perfect, as might be expected from Fiona, as she could tell from everything Creed had said about his aunt.

Her stomach jumped, nervous, and a slight storm of nausea rose inside her. Aberdeen put her toast down. "It's delicious, Fiona."

Fiona beamed. It *was* delicious. If Aberdeen had eaten it at any other time in her life, she'd want to hop in the kitchen and learn Fiona's secrets. There were probably secrets involved in making something this tasty, secrets that could only be passed from one cook to another. Her stomach slithered around, catching her by surprise. She felt strangely like an interloper, a case taken on by these wonderful people and Creed. That wasn't the way she wanted to feel.

And then he walked into the kitchen, big and tall and filling the doorway, her own John Wayne in the flesh, and sunshine flooded Aberdeen in a way she'd never felt before.

"It's wonderful jam," Diane said, and Aberdeen nodded, never taking her eyes off the cowboy she'd come to love. He grinned at her, oblivious to her worries, and if she didn't know better, she would have thought his eyes held a special twinkle for her. Ashley got down from her chair and tottered over to him to be swept up into his arms. Lincoln Rose and Suzanne sat in their high chairs, patiently waiting for their turns for attention from Creed. Creed walked over and blew a tiny raspberry against Lincoln Rose's cheek, making her giggle, and did the same to Suzanne. They waved their baby spoons, delighted with the attention.

Then Creed winked at Aberdeen, in lieu of a good-morning kiss, and Aberdeen forced a smile back, trying to sail along on the boat of Unexpected Good Fortune.

But life wasn't all blue-ribbon strawberry jam and gold-scrolling placards. At least not her life.

Diane poked her in the arm, and Aberdeen tried to be more perky. More happy. More perfect.

She felt like such a fraud.

Chapter Fifteen

Pete and Jackie strolled in, carrying their three babies and a flotilla of baby gear, and the mood in the kitchen lifted instantly. Creed rose to help his brother and sister-in-law settle themselves at the breakfast table.

"We figured there'd be grub," Pete said, "hope you don't mind us joining you, Aunt Fiona."

She gave him a light smack on the arm with a wooden spoon. "The more, the merrier, I always say." She beamed and went back to stirring things up on the stove. Jackie seated herself next to Aberdeen.

"So, how do you feel about the royal treatment, Aberdeen?" Jackie asked.

"It's amazing. Truly." Aberdeen caught Creed's smile at her compliment. "Jackie, Pete, I'd like you to meet my sister, Diane."

Diane smiled, shaking her head at the babies Pete and Jackie were trying to get settled in their baby carriers. "I had my babies one at a time and I still felt like it was a lot. I can't imagine it happening all at once."

Jackie smiled. "We couldn't, either. And then it did." She got a grin from her proud husband, and Aberdeen's gaze once again shifted to Creed. He seemed completely unafraid of all the babies crowding in around him—in fact, he seemed happy.

"It hasn't been bad," Pete said. "We're catching on faster than I thought we would. Jackie's a quick study."

Aberdeen didn't think she'd be a quick study. She pushed her toast around on her plate, trying to eat, wishing the nausea would pass. She caught Creed looking at her, and he winked at her again, seeming to know that she was plagued by doubts. Cold chills ran across her skin. She didn't think she'd be radiant sunshine like Jackie if she found herself with three newborn triplets. He'd probably be dismally disappointed if she didn't take to mothering like a duck to water. "Excuse me," she said, getting up from the table, feeling slightly wan, "I'm going to find a powder room."

"I'll show you," Jackie said, quickly getting up to lead her down a hall.

"Thanks," Aberdeen said, definitely not feeling like herself.

"You look a bit peaked. Are you feeling all right?" Jackie asked.

"I'm fine. Thank you." Aberdeen tried to smile. But then she wasn't, and she flew into the powder room, and when she came back out a few moments later, Jackie was waiting, seated on a chair in the wide hallway.

"Maybe not so fine?" Jackie said.

"I suppose not." Embarrassment flashed over her. "I've always been a good traveler. I can't imagine what's come over me."

"Hmm. Let's sit down and rest for a minute before we go back to the kitchen."

Aberdeen sat, gratefully.

"It can be overwhelming here, at first."

"I think you're right." Aberdeen nodded. "Johnny and I live a much simpler life. And yet, everyone here is so nice."

"Did you know your sister was coming?"

Aberdeen shook her head.

"Well, you've got a lot going on." Jackie patted her hand. "Let me know if there's anything I can do to help."

"You have three newborns." Aberdeen realized the nausea had passed for the moment. "I should be helping you."

"We all help each other." Jackie looked at her. "Your color is returning. Are you feeling better? You were so pale when you left the kitchen."

"I feel much better. I've always been very fortunate with my health. I don't think I've had more than a few colds in my life, and I'm never sick. I can't imagine what's come over me." Aberdeen wondered if she was getting cold feet. But she wouldn't get cold about Creed. He made her feel hotter than a firecracker.

"Not that's it's any of my business," Jackie said, "but the nurse in me wonders if you might be pregnant?"

Aberdeen laughed. "Oh, no. Not at all. There's no way." Then the smile slipped slowly off her face as she remembered.

There *was* a way.

Jackie grinned at her. Aberdeen shook her head. "I'm pretty certain I'm not."

"Okay." Jackie nodded. "Can you face the breakfast table?"

Aberdeen wasn't certain. Her stomach pitched slightly. "I think so."

Jackie watched her as she stood. "You don't have to eat breakfast, you know. It's a lovely time of the day to take a walk in the fresh air. And I'd be happy to keep an eye on your little ones."

"I think...I think I might take your suggestion." Something about the smell of eggs and coffee was putting her off. She felt that she'd be better off heading outside until her stomach righted itself. "I'm sure it's nothing, but...would you mind letting Fiona know I'm going to head back to the guest house?"

"Absolutely." Jackie showed her to a side door. "Don't worry about a thing."

Aberdeen *was* worried, about a lot of things.

I can't be pregnant. I was in the safe zone of the month when we—

She walked outside, the early-morning sunshine kissing her skin, lifting the nausea. "No, I'm not," she told herself, reassuringly.

A baby would really complicate matters. As wonderful as Rancho Diablo was, Aberdeen felt as though she was on vacation—not at home. Being here was fairy-tale-ish—complete with a villain or two—and any moment she should wake up.

She didn't know how to tell Creed that as much as she wanted to keep to their bargain, she didn't know if she could.

CREED GLANCED UP when Jackie came back into the kitchen, his brows rising. "Where's Aberdeen?"

Jackie seated herself, looking at him with a gentle smile. "She's taking a little walk. Fiona, she said to tell you she'd see you in a bit." Jackie smiled at her husband, and resumed eating, as though everything was just fine and dandy.

But Creed knew it wasn't. Jackie had high marks in

this family for her ability to cover things up—look at how skillfully she'd gotten Pete to the altar. So Creed's instinctive radar snapped on. "Is she all right?"

"She's fine."

Jackie didn't meet his eyes as she nibbled on some toast. "Maybe I'll go join her on that walk," he said, and Diane said, "Good idea."

Jackie waved a hand. "I think she said she was looking forward to some solitude."

That was the signal. It just didn't sound like something Aberdeen would say. Creed got to his feet. "I think I'll go check on the horses."

Diane nodded. "My girls and I are going to sit here and enjoy some more of this delicious breakfast." She whisked her sister's abandoned plate to the sink. "Fiona, if I could cook half as well as you do, I might still have a husband."

Fiona grinned. "You think?"

"No." Diane laughed. "But I would have eaten better."

Diane seemed comfortable with Fiona and company, much more so than Aberdeen did. Creed got to his feet. "I'll be back, Aunt Fiona."

"All right." His aunt beamed at him, and Creed escaped, trying not to run after Aberdeen as he caught sight of her walking toward the guest house. "Hey," he said. "A girl as pretty as you shouldn't be walking alone."

Aberdeen gave him a slight, barely-there-and-mostly-fakey smile. Creed blinked. "Are you okay, Aberdeen?"

"I'm fine. Really."

"Hey." He caught her hand, slowing her down. "You trying to run away from me, lady?"

She shook her head. "I just need a little time to myself." She took her hands from his, gazing at him with apology in her eyes.

"Oh." Creed nodded. "All right." He didn't feel good about the sound of that. "Call me if you need anything. Burke keeps the guest house stocked pretty well, but—"

"I'm fine, Creed. Thank you."

And then she turned and hurried off, smiting his ego. *Damn.* Creed watched her go, unsure of what had just happened. He wanted to head after her, pry some answers out of her, but a man couldn't do a woman that way. They needed space sometimes.

He just wished the space she seemed to need didn't have to be so far away from him.

ABERDEEN FELT GUILTY about disappearing on Fiona, and Diane—and Creed. She didn't want to be rude, but she wanted to wash up, change her clothes, shower. Think. Just a few moments to catch her breath and think about what she was doing.

She felt like she was on the Tilt-A-Whirl at the State Fair, and she couldn't stop whirling.

At least I'm not pregnant, she told herself. *I'm a planner. Planning makes me feel organized, secure.*

I've got to focus.

"Hey," Johnny called, spying her. "Wait up."

He caught up to her, following her into the guest house. "It feels like I haven't seen you in days."

"That's because we're in this suspended twilight of Happyville." Aberdeen went into the bathroom to wash up. When she came out, Johnny was lounging in the common area.

"That didn't sound particularly happy, if we're hanging out in Happyville." Johnny shot her a worried look. "What's up?"

Aberdeen sat on one of the leather sofas opposite Johnny. "I don't know, exactly."

He nodded. "Feel like you're on vacation and shouldn't be?"

"Maybe." Aberdeen considered that. "I need to wake up."

"An engagement, three kids that aren't yours, a new place…" His voice drifted off as he gazed around the room. "Saying yes to a guy who lives in a mansion would freak me out, I guess, if I was a woman."

"Why?" Aberdeen asked, and Johnny grinned.

"Because your bar was set too low. Re-ride wasn't much of a comparison, you know?"

Aberdeen nodded. "I lost my breakfast, and Jackie wanted to know if I was pregnant."

"Oh, wow." Johnny laughed. "That would be crazy."

Aberdeen glared at him.

"Oh, wait," Johnny said, "is there a possibility I could be an uncle again?"

"I don't think so," Aberdeen snapped, and Johnny raised a brow.

"That's not a ringing endorsement of your birth-control method."

Aberdeen sighed. "I don't want to talk about it." The best thing to do was to concentrate, and right now, she just wanted to concentrate on what was going on with Diane. "Johnny, have you noticed that Diane seems to like her children just fine?"

"Mmm. She's just not comfortable with them. She's like Mom."

Aberdeen felt a stab of worry. "I wonder if I'd be like that."

Johnny crooked a brow. "You're not pregnant, so don't worry about it. Unless you might be pregnant, and then don't worry about it. You're nothing like Mom and Diane."

"How do you know? How does any mother know?" Aberdeen was scared silly at the very thought that she might bring a child into the world she couldn't bond with.

"Because," Johnny said, "you're different. You were always different. You cared about people. I love Diane, but she pretty much cares about herself, and whatever's going on in her world. You had a congregation that loved you, Aberdeen."

Aberdeen blinked. "I miss it. Maybe that's what's wrong with me."

"Well, I don't think that's all that's going on with you, but—" Johnny shrugged. "The pattern of your life has been completely interrupted. The bright side is that you can build a congregation here, if you want. I'm sure there's always a need for a cowboy preacher."

Aberdeen wasn't certain she wanted a new church. "What if I want my old church? My old way of life?" she asked softly.

Johnny looked at her. "I think that bridge has been crossed and burned behind us, sis."

Creed burst in the door, halting when he saw Johnny and Aberdeen chatting. He was carrying a brown paper bag, which caught Aberdeen's suspicious gaze.

"Sorry," Creed said, "Didn't realize you two were visiting."

"It's all right," Johnny said. "I'm just taking a break

from ranching. I think I'm getting the hang of this cowboy gig." He waved a hand at the paper bag. "Did you bring us breakfast or liquor?"

Creed set the bag on a chair. "Neither."

Aberdeen shot her fiancé a guarded look. "Is that what I think it is, Creed Callahan?"

"I don't think so," Creed said. "It's a…lunch for me. That's what it is. I packed myself a lunch."

"You're going to go hungry, then," Johnny observed. "You can't work on a ranch and eat a lunch the size of an apple."

"It's for me," Aberdeen guessed.

"It's for us," Creed said, and Johnny got to his feet.

"I'll leave you two lovebirds alone," he said, and Aberdeen didn't tell him to stay.

"Goodbye," Johnny said, and went out the door.

"Creed, that's a drugstore bag," Aberdeen said, "and since you just bought a huge box of condoms when we were in Wyoming, I'm betting you bought a pregnancy test."

He looked sheepish. "How'd you guess?"

"Because you looked scared when you ran in here, like your world was on fire. Jackie told you, didn't she?"

"Well, everyone was worried. We thought something was really wrong with you. And Fiona started fretting, worrying that you didn't like her food, and Jackie said it was a girl thing, and she'd tell Fiona later, and then Diane blurted out that maybe you were pregnant, and I—" He looked like a nervous father-to-be. "Could you be?"

"I don't think so." Aberdeen sighed. "I mean, I guess it's possible. But not likely."

"It wasn't likely for Pete to have triplets, either," Creed said. "Maybe we'd better find out."

"I don't have to pee," Aberdeen said, feeling belligerent. She didn't want everyone at Rancho Diablo discussing her life.

"I'll get you a glass of water," Creed said, jumping to his feet, and Aberdeen said, "No!"

"Well, I might get a glass of water for me. With ice. It's hot in here."

Aberdeen closed her eyes. Just the thought of being a dad clearly was making him nervous. He'd have four children, Aberdeen realized, all at once.

"It wouldn't be what we agreed on," Aberdeen said, and Creed said, "We'll make a new agreement. After I drink a tall glass of water." He went into the kitchen and turned the faucet on full-blast. "Do you hear water running, sweetheart?"

Aberdeen shook her head. "I'm not going to take the test."

He shut off the faucet and came back in with a glass of water. "We'll drink together."

"You pee in the cup." Aberdeen ignored the glass Creed set beside her.

"I didn't get a cup," Creed said cheerfully. "I bought the stick one. It looked more efficient. And it said it could detect a pregnancy five or six days before a skipped—"

Aberdeen swiped the bag from him. "I'm not going to do it while you're here."

"Why not?" Creed was puzzled.

"Because," Aberdeen said. "I need privacy. I have a shy bladder."

He grinned at her. "No, you don't. I happen to know there's nothing shy about you, my little wildcat."

Aberdeen looked at him, her blood pressure rising. "I just want to avoid the topic a little while longer, all right?"

"Well, I feel like a kid on my birthday trying to decide which present to open first," Creed told her. "Pregnancy will probably be a very healthy thing for me."

"Is this about the ranch?" Aberdeen asked, and Creed looked wounded.

"No," he said, "that's dumb."

"Why? You said yourself—"

"I know." Creed held up a hand. "I told you getting married was about getting the ranch. I'd have three built-in daughters, and it would get Fiona off my back. I told you all that, it's true. But it's not anymore."

She looked at him, wanting to kiss him. Maybe he was falling for her as hard as she was falling for him! "What is it, then?"

"Our agreement?" Creed considered her question. "I don't know. Grab the pee stick and we'll renegotiate based on whether you come up yes or no." He rubbed his palms together. "It's almost as much fun as a magic eight ball."

Aberdeen closed her eyes for a second, counting to ten. "Did anyone ever tell you you're a goof?"

"No. They just call me handsome. And devil-may-care." He came to sit next to her with his icy glass of water. "Drink, sweetpea?"

Chapter Sixteen

Twenty minutes later, Creed tapped on the bathroom door. It seemed like Aberdeen had been in there a long time. "Aberdeen? Are you taking a nap in there?"

"Give me a second," she said, and he wondered if her voice sounded teary. Was she crying?

His heart rate skyrocketed. "Let me in."

"No."

"Is something wrong?"

"I don't think so."

He blinked. That sounded foreboding, he decided. "Do you want your sister?"

"No, thank you."

He pondered his next attack. She couldn't be in there all day. He was about to relinquish his sentinel position outside her door when it opened.

Aberdeen walked out, and he saw at once that she *had* been crying. "Guess we're having a baby?"

She nodded.

He opened his arms, and she walked into them, her body shaking. Creed held her, and she sniffled a second against his chest, and then she pulled away.

He wanted her back. "I'm really amping up the pressure on my brothers," he said cheerfully, seeing a whole world of possibilities kaleidoscoping before him. He'd have a son to play ball with, to teach how to ride. Was there anything better than a boy to help him on the ranch?

Even if they didn't have a ranch anymore, he'd have a son.

"Aberdeen, sweetie, this is the best news I've had in my entire life. Thank you."

She looked at him. "Really?"

"Oh, hell, yeah." He sat down, checking his gut and knew every word he was speaking was true. "I feel like a superhero."

She wiped at her eyes, then looked at him with a giggle. "I feel strangely like a villainess."

"Uh-uh." He shook his head. "I mean, you're sexy and all, but there's nothing evil about you, babe, except maybe what you do to my sense of self-control. I don't suppose you'd like to have a celebratory quickie?"

She laughed but shook her head.

"It was worth a try." He liked seeing the smile on her face. "Hey, you know what this means, don't you?"

"It means a lot of things. Name the topic."

He felt about ten feet tall in his boots. "We need to plan a wedding."

She looked at him, surprised. "Isn't that rushing things a bit?"

"Not for me. I'm an eight-second guy. I'm all about speed and staying on my ride."

Aberdeen crossed her arms in a protective gesture, almost hugging herself. "When I met you, you hadn't stayed on your ride. In fact, you had a concussion. What if—"

"What if I decide to bail?" He grinned at her and

pulled her into his lap. "Lady, you're just going to have to stick around to find out."

She looked down at him from her perch. "I'm way over my head here, cowboy. Just so you know."

"Nah. This is going to be a piece of cake. Fiona can help you plan a wedding. Or we can elope. Whichever you prefer." He nibbled on her neck. "Personally, I'd pick eloping. We'll get to sleep together faster. And you'll make a cute Mrs. Callahan. I'm going to chase my Mrs. Callahan around for the rest of my life."

"I can run fast."

"I know," he said, "but I think we just learned that I run faster."

She laughed, and he kissed her, glad to see the waterworks had shut off. She'd scared him! No man wanted to think that the mother of his child didn't want him. But he was pretty certain Aberdeen did want him, just as much as he wanted her. It was just taking her a little longer to decide that she wanted him for the long haul.

He wasn't letting her get away from him. "When are you going to make an announcement?"

She sighed. "I think something was foreshadowed when you ran in here with a paper bag from the drugstore. I won't be surprised if Fiona has already ordered a nursery. And I don't even know anything about you." For a moment, she looked panicked. "You know more about me than I do about you."

He shrugged. "No mysteries here. Ask a question."

"Okay." Aberdeen pulled back slightly when he tried to nibble at her bottom lip. Maybe if he got her mind off the pregnancy, he could ease her into bed. He did his best romancing between the sheets, he was pretty certain. Right now, her brain was on overdrive, processing, and if she only but knew it, he could massage her and kiss her body into a puddle of relaxation. He felt himself getting very intrigued by the thought.

"Who's the scary guy who visited?" Aberdeen asked. "That Bode guy?"

Uh-oh. It was going to be hard to lure her into a compromising position if she was up for difficult topics. "He's just the local wacko. No one special."

"I felt like I'd been visited by the evil Rancho Diablo spirit."

He sighed, realizing he was getting nothing at the moment—even his powers of romance weren't up to combating a woman who was still trying to figure out if she wanted to be tied to his family, friends and enemies. "I'm a very eligible bachelor," he said, "you don't have to examine the skeletons in my closet. Why don't we hop down to Jackie's bridal shop and look at dresses?" he said. Surely if romance wouldn't do it, shopping might get her thinking about weddings—and a future with him.

"Bode Jenkins," she said. "Was he threatening me?"

"He was being a pest. We're used to him showing up uninvited, trying to throw a wrench into things. Don't take it personally."

"He wants your ranch."

"Yep." Creed shrugged. "I think he may be delusional. He doesn't really want the ranch. He just wants to stick it to us. That's my personal assessment." He nuzzled at her cheek. "I'll be a lot stronger in my fight against evil and doom if I'm married. Let's talk about our future, all right?"

She moved away from his mouth. "Quit trying to seduce me. You're trying to get me off topic, and it isn't going to work."

He sighed. "Most women in your shoes would be more than happy to talk about tying me down, sister."

She took a long time to answer, and when she did, it wasn't what he wanted to hear. "I can't get married at the snap of a finger, Creed. Mom and Dad would want me to get married at home—"

"We can fly them here."

"They would want me to have a church wedding—"

"But what do you want?" he asked, wondering why she was suddenly so worried about her parents. Her folks didn't seem to be all that interested in what she did. He moved his lips along her arm, pondering this new turn of events.

"I don't know. I just found out I'm having a baby. I can't really think about a wedding right now." She slid out of his lap and walked over to the window. "I'd better get back to the girls. I've left them alone too long."

"They're not alone," Creed said, surprised. "They're with their mothe—"

The glare she shot him would have knocked him back two feet if he'd been standing. She went out the door like a storm, and Creed realized he had a whole lot of convincing to do to get his bride to the altar.

In fact, it was probably going to take a miracle.

"I NEVER THOUGHT it would be so difficult to get a woman to jump into a wedding gown," Creed told his twin a few minutes later, when Rafe sat down next to him in the barn. Creed still felt stunned by the whirling turn of events in his life. "I'm going to be a father. I want to be a husband. I don't want my son coming to me one day and saying, "Mom says you were half-baked with the marriage proposal." He looked at Rafe. "You know what I mean?"

Rafe shook his head. "Nope."

Creed sighed, looking at the bridle he was repairing. Trying to repair. This should have been mental cotton candy for him, and he was muffing the repair job. His concentration was shot. "Imagine finding out the best news in your life, but the person who's giving you the news acts like you're radioactive. You would feel pretty low."

"Yeah. But I'm not you. I'd just make her say yes."

Creed looked at Rafe. "Thanks for the body-blow."

Rafe grinned and took the bridle from him. "Give her some time, bro. She's just beginning to figure out that you've turned her life inside out. She needs some time to adjust."

"Yeah," Creed said, "but I want her to be Mrs. Callahan before I have to roll her down the aisle in a wheelbarrow."

Rafe looked at him. "And you wonder why Aberdeen isn't running a four-minute mile to get to the altar with you. Is that the way you romance a woman? 'Honey, let's get hitched before my brawny son expands your waistline?'"

"I never said a word about that. I just want sooner rather than later. I don't really care if she's the size of an elephant, I just want her wearing white lace pronto." Creed scratched his head, and shoved his hat back. "Truthfully, I think I wanted to marry that gal the moment I laid eyes on her. Even in my debilitated state, I knew I'd stumbled on something awesome." He looked at Rafe. "Aberdeen *is* awesome."

Rafe considered him. "You really are crazy about her, aren't you? This isn't about the ranch for you."

"Nope. I've tried every song-and-dance routine I know to get her to take me on. I've offered short-term marriage, marriage-of-convenience, and the real deal. She just doesn't set a date." He sighed, feeling worn down. "It's killing me. I really think I'm aging. And I'm pretty sure it's supposed to be the woman who plots to get the guy to wedded bliss. She sure can drag her feet."

"I don't know, man. All I know is you better shape up before the big dance tomorrow night."

Creed straightened. "That's not tomorrow night, is it?"

Rafe nodded.

"Oh, hell. I've got a bad feeling about this."

Aberdeen already seemed overwhelmed by the ranch, by Rancho Diablo, by him. How would she feel about a bachelor ball? He already knew. She would see his brothers hooting and hollering, trying to catch women and vice versa, and figure that he was no different from those lunkheads. That's how a woman thought. "I bet pregnant women probably jump to conclusions faster than normal, because of their hormones and stuff."

Rafe smacked him on the head. "Of the two of us, you are definitely the dumbest. Why do you talk like Aberdeen has no common sense? When beautiful, husband-hunting women are throwing themselves at you tomorrow night, she'll totally understand. It'll probably make her want you. Jealousy is catnip to a woman."

Creed groaned. If he knew Aberdeen the way he thought he did, she was going to run for the mountains of Wyoming. She was like a piece of dry tinder just waiting for a spark to set her off. He could feel her looking for reasons not to trust him. Damn Re-ride, he thought. He'd convinced her that all men were rats.

"Most men are rats," he said, pondering out loud, and Rafe nodded.

"Very likely. And women still love us."

Creed didn't think Aberdeen was going to love him if she could convince herself that he was a big stinky rodent. "I've got to get her out of here," he said, but his twin just shrugged.

"Good luck," Rafe said, and Creed figured he'd need a turnaround in his luck pattern if he wanted his bride.

He knew just who could advise him.

DIANE SAT ON a porch swing, watching her daughters play in a huge sandbox the brothers had constructed for all the new babies at Rancho Diablo. Maybe it was dumb, Creed thought, to make a sandbox when the babies were all still, well, babies. Ashley and Suzu were big enough to play in the soft sand dotted with toys, but Lincoln Rose would catch up in time, and so would Pete's daughters.

Creed couldn't wait to see all the kids playing together one day. The vista of Rancho Diablo land made a beautiful backdrop for children to view, panoramic and Hollywood-like. Burke had helped, drawing off precise measurements and finding the best type of sand to make wonderful castles.

And now Diane sat on the porch swing alone, watching her two oldest, and holding her baby. He watched her for a second, and then went to join the woman he hoped would be his sister-in-law one day.

"Hi," he said, and Diane turned her head.

"Hello."

"Mind if I join you?"

"Not at all. Please do." She smiled when he sat down. "My girls really like it here. There's something about this ranch that seems to agree with them."

He nodded. "It was a pretty great place to grow up."

Diane looked back at her girls. Creed realized her gaze was following her daughters with interest, not the almost cursory, maybe even scared expression she'd worn before.

"Are you comfortable here?" Creed asked.

"I am." She nodded. "Your aunt and uncle have been very kind."

Creed started to say that Burke wasn't his uncle, then decided the tag was close enough. Burke was fatherly, more than uncle-like, and a dear friend. "How long are you staying?"

She smiled, keeping her gaze on her daughters. Creed mentally winced, his question sounding abrupt to him. He sure didn't want Diane to think he was trying to run her off.

"Your aunt has offered me a job," Diane said, surprising Creed.

"She has?"

"Mmm." She turned to look at him, and he saw that her eyes were just like Aberdeen's and Johnny's, deep and blue and beautiful. But hers were lined with years of worry. She'd had it hard, he realized—no wonder Aberdeen and Johnny were so bent on helping her. "She says she needs a housekeeper/assistant. She says all her duties are getting to be too much for her. Yet your Aunt Fiona seems quite energetic to me."

Creed shrugged. "I wouldn't blame Fiona a bit if she felt like she needed some help. She's got an awful lot she does on the ranch."

"So it wasn't just a polite invitation?" Diane looked at him curiously.

"I doubt it. While my aunt is unfailingly polite, she's never offered such a position to anyone else that I'm aware of, and she wouldn't fancy giving up any of the reins of the place if she really didn't feel the need." He smiled. "She's pretty fierce about doing everything herself."

"So why me? Because I'm Aberdeen's sister?"

He shrugged again. "Probably because she likes you. Fiona prefers to run her own business, so if she offered, she must have felt that you'd be an asset to the ranch."

"She doesn't discuss hiring with you?"

He laughed. "She may have talked to some of my brothers. I can't say. But Fiona's business is her own. So if you're interested in a job with her, that's a discussion between the two of you. The only tip I could positively give you is that if you accept her offer, you will work harder than you ever have in your life. Ask Burke if you don't believe me."

She finally smiled. "I'll think about it, then."

"Yeah. Well, glad I could help. Not that I have any useful information to impart." He grinned at the pile of sand the two little girls were pushing around in the box with the aid of a tiny tractor and some shovels. "So now I have a question for you."

"All right," Diane said. "You want to know how I can help you to get Aberdeen to marry you."

He blinked. "Well, if you could, it would help."

She smiled. "Look, Creed. I'm going to be just as honest with you as you were with me. Aberdeen doesn't always talk about what she's thinking. If she does, she'd go to Johnny first, and then maybe she'd come to me. I'm a lot older than Aberdeen, in many ways. But I can tell you a couple of things. First, she's afraid she's turning out like me. The fact that she's pregnant makes it feel real unplanned to her, for lack of a better word, and Aberdeen is all about planning everything very seriously. People who plan are *responsible.* Do you understand what I'm saying?" She gave him a long, sideways look.

Creed nodded. "Thank you for your honesty."

She went back to watching her daughters. "It's good to self-examine, even when it's painful. I know who I am, and I know what I'm not. I'm not a good mother, but I know I'm a good person. That probably doesn't make sense to you, but I know that in the end, the good person in me will triumph."

Creed thought she was probably right. There was a kind streak in Diane, a part of her that acknowledged strength in family, that he'd already noticed. "No one's perfect," he said. "Neither my brothers nor I would claim we've come within a spitting distance of perfect. So you're probably amongst like-minded people."

Diane placed a soft kiss atop Lincoln Rose's head. Creed wondered if she even realized she'd done it. "Back to Aberdeen. The B-part to my sister that I know and understand—though I'm not claiming to be an expert— is that there will never be another Re-ride in her life."

"I'm no Re-ride," he growled.

"I mean that, even if she married Re-ride again, it would be no retread situation. Aberdeen is not the same shy girl who got married so young. She would kick his butt from here to China if she married him and he tried to do the stupid stuff he did before."

"She's not marrying Re-ride," Creed said decisively,

"and I'm no green boy for her to be worrying about marrying."

Diane sighed. "I'm sure Aberdeen is well aware that it was a real man who put a ring on her finger this time, cowboy. All I'm saying is that she's going to make her own decisions in her life now. She'll do things when she's comfortable and not before—and right now, I'd say she's not totally comfortable. Some of that is probably due to me, but—" She gave Creed a long look and stood. "I feel pretty comfortable in saying that most of her indecision is due to you," she said, kissing him on the cheek, "future brother-in-law."

He looked at her. "I don't wait well."

She smiled. "I guessed that. You may have to this time, if you really want your bride." Diane went to the sandbox and said, "Girls, we need to get washed up now," and they dutifully minded their mother. Creed watched with astonishment as they followed Diane like little ducklings. It was one of the most beautiful things he'd ever seen. He wondered if Diane had yet realized that she had no reason to be afraid of being a mother—she seemed to have all the proper components except confidence. He watched the girls go with a little bit of sentimental angst, already considering himself their father in his heart, knowing that they needed their mother, too. He'd have thought Lincoln Rose would have at least reached for him.

But no. They'd been content to spend time with their mother, an invisible natural bond growing into place. Creed wished he could grow some kind of bond with Aberdeen. She seemed determined to dissolve what they had. "I'm not doing this right," he muttered, and jumped when Burke said, "Did you say something, Creed?"

Creed glanced behind him as Fiona's butler materialized with a tray of lemonade and cookies. "Are those for me?"

"They're for the little girls and their mother." Burke glanced around. "Are they done with play time?"

"I'm afraid so. Bring that tray over here to me. I need fortification."

Burke set the tray down on the porch swing.

"There's only one glass," Creed said.

"Yes. The lemonade is for you. It has a little kick in it, which I noticed you looked like you needed about twenty minutes ago when you ran through the house."

Creed looked at Burke. "Okay. Tell me everything you're dying to say."

"I'm not really an advice column," Burke said. "I see my role more as fortifier."

Creed waved a hand, knocking back half the lemonade. "You're right. That does have a kick. And it's just what I needed."

Burke nodded. "The cookies are for the girls. They get milk with theirs, usually."

Creed blinked. "Well, my ladies have departed me. All of them, I fear."

Burke cleared his throat. "If you don't need anything else—"

"Actually, I think I do." Creed looked at the butler, considering him. "Burke, your secret is out. We all know you and Fiona are married."

Burke remained silent, staring at him with no change in expression.

Creed let out a sigh. "I guess my question is, how did you do it?"

"How did I do what?"

"How did you convince my aunt to get to the altar?"

Burke picked up the tray. "I sense the topic you're exploring is Miss Aberdeen."

"I could use some advice. Yes." Creed nodded. "Wise men seek counsel when needed, Burke, and I know you have some experience with handling an independent-minded female. My problem is that I've got a woman who seems a little more cold-footed than the average female, when it comes to getting to the altar."

"I may have mentioned my role isn't giving advice," Burke said, "but if I had any, I would say that the lady in question seems to know her own mind. Therefore, she undoubtedly will not take well to being pushed." Burke handed him a cookie. "I must go find the young ladies. It's past time for their afternoon snack and nap."

Creed nodded. "Thanks, Burke."

The butler disappeared.

"I'm not hearing anything I want to hear," Creed muttered. "I know a woman needs her space. But I'm no Re-ride." He munched on the cookie, thinking it would taste better if Aberdeen was there to share it with him.

Between Burke's special lemonade, the cookie and the advice, he thought he was starting to feel better. Not much, just a little, but better all the same.

He was going to be a father.

He wanted to be a husband, too.

He wanted Aberdeen like nothing he'd ever wanted in his life. If his aunt had sprung the perfect woman on him, she couldn't have chosen better. He would easily trade Rancho Diablo if Aberdeen would be his wife. He wanted to spend the rest of his days lying in bed with her, holding her, touching her.

He was just going to have to hang on.

Chapter Seventeen

"I'm worried about Sabrina McKinley," Fiona said to Creed when he rolled into the kitchen. She was making a pie, blueberry, he was pretty sure.

For once, he had no appetite for Fiona's baking. "You mean because of Bode?"

"Well, I certainly didn't like his tone the other night. He made it sound like she was a prisoner or something. The man gives me the creeps." She shook her head and placed the pie on a cooling rack. "I begin to rethink my plan of planting her, I really do, Creed."

"Jonas checked on her. He'd know if something was wrong." Creed sometimes wondered if his oldest brother had developed a secret penchant for Fiona's spy. Then he dismissed that. Jonas was nothing if not boring. He'd never go for the Mata Hari type.

"I suppose." She fluffed her hands off over the sink, brightening. "On the other hand, we have news to celebrate!"

"Yeah." Creed didn't know how his aunt always managed to hear everything lightning-fast. "I'm going to be a father." He beamed, just saying the words a pleasure.

Fiona's mouth dropped open. "You're having a baby?"

He nodded. "Isn't that the news you were talking about?"

She slowly shook her head. "I was going to say that we have one hundred and fifty beautiful, eligible bachelorettes attending the ball tomorrow night." Her gaze was glued to him. "Is the mother Aberdeen?" she asked, almost whispering.

"Yes!" He stared at his aunt, startled. "Who else would it be?"

"How would I know?" Fiona demanded. "You were gone for months. I thought you had only just met Aberdeen when you got thrown off the last bull."

He nodded. "Absolutely all correct."

"That means you two got friendly awfully *quickly.*" She peered at him, her gaze steadfast. "Goodness, you've barely given the poor girl a chance to breathe! No wonder she left."

He blinked. "Left?"

Fiona hesitated, her eyes searching his. "Didn't she tell you?"

His heart began an uncomfortable pounding in his chest. "Tell me what?"

"That she was going back home? She left an hour ago."

Creed sat down heavily in a kitchen chair. Then he sprang up, unable to sit, his muscles bunched with tension. "She didn't say a word."

"I think she said something about a letter. Burke!"

Her butler/secret husband popped into the kitchen. "Yes?"

"When Aberdeen thanked us for our hospitality and said she was leaving, did she leave a letter of some kind?"

Burke's gaze moved to Creed. "She did. I am not to give it to Creed until six o'clock this evening."

"The hell with that," Creed said, "give it to me now."

Burke shook his head. "I cannot. It was entrusted to me with certain specifications."

Creed felt his jaw tightening, his teeth grinding as he stared at the elderly man prepared to stick to his principles at all costs. "Burke, remember the chat we had a little while ago out back?"

Burke nodded.

"And you know I'm crazy about that woman?"

Burke nodded.

"Then give me the letter so that I can stop her," Creed said, "please."

Burke said. "Creed, you're like a son to me. But I can't go against a promise."

"Damn it!" Creed exclaimed.

Fiona and Burke stared at him, their eyes round with compassion and sympathy.

"I apologize," Creed said. He ran rough hands through his hair. His muscles seemed to lose form suddenly, so he collapsed in a chair. "I don't suppose she said why?" he asked Fiona.

Fiona shook her head. "She said she needed to be back home. I asked her to stay for the ball, and she said she felt she'd only be underfoot. However," she said brightly, "Diane, Johnny and the girls stayed."

"Good," Creed said, shooting to his feet, "I've got a future brother-in-law to go pound."

"He's a guest!" Fiona called after him. "He saved your life!"

Creed strode out to find Johnny—and some answers.

FIVE HOURS LATER, at exactly six o'clock—and after learning that Johnny and Diane knew nothing at all about Aberdeen's departure—Burke finally presented Aberdeen's letter to Creed, formally, on a silver platter.

The envelope was white, the cursive writing black and ladylike. Creed tore it open, aware that his family was watching his every move. News of Aberdeen's departure—and pregnancy—had spread like wildfire through Rancho Diablo. No one had had a clue that Aberdeen had wanted to leave.

Of course he'd known. In his heart, he'd known she was questioning their relationship from the minute she'd seen the ranch and the jet to the moment she'd learned she was pregnant.

Creed, I want you to know how sorry I am that I will be unable to keep our bargain. As you know, at the time we made it, I was under the belief that Diane wanted me to adopt her children. I had no idea when, or if, Diane might return. But now I am hopeful that, given a little more time with her daughters and the gentle comfort of Rancho Diablo, my sister is gaining a true desire and appreciation of what it means to be a mother. This is more than I could have ever hoped for. For that reason, I'm leaving her here, in good hands, as Fiona has offered her employment. I know Diane is happy here, happier than I might ever be. It seems a fair trade-off.

My part of the bargain to you was that marriage might cure your aunt's desire to see you married to help keep Rancho Diablo. I don't think you'll need my help. All of you seem quite determined to keep fighting, and I pray for the best for you. Mr. Jenkins seems most disagreeable, so I hope the good guys win. After the ball tomorrow night, perhaps all of your brothers will find wonderful wives. That is something else I will be praying for.

As you know, I have a congregation and a life back in Lance that means a lot to me. When I met you, I believed you were basically an itinerant cowboy. Marrying you for your name on an adoption application didn't seem all that wrong, considering that you, too, had a need of marriage. Now that I've met your family, I know that it would be wrong for me to marry you under false pretenses. That's just not the kind of person I am. Yours is a different kind of lifestyle than I could ever live up to. In the end, though you are a wonderful, solid man, I realize that my life and your life are just too different. With Diane finding her footing with her girls, I think this is a happy ending. I have you and your family to thank for that. So I'd say that any debt that may have existed before is certainly wiped out.

I know too well that you will want visitation rights once the baby is born. You no doubt have lawyers available to you who can draw up any documents you wish to that effect.

I know we will be talking in the future about our child's welfare, so I hope we can remain friends.

All my best,

Aberdeen

P.S. I have entrusted Burke with the engagement ring. Thank you so much for the gesture. For a while, I did feel like a real fiancée.

He looked up from the letter, his heart shattered. "She left me," he said, and his brothers seemed to sink down in their various chairs.

The silence in the room was long and hard. No one knew what to say to him. His hands shook as he stared at the letter again. She didn't feel like a real fiancée.

How could she not? Had he not loved her every chance he got? "She says she didn't feel like a real bride-to-be," he murmured. "But she's having my baby. How can she not feel like she's going to be a real wife?"

Jonas cleared his throat. "Women get strange sometimes when they're pregnant," he said, and Fiona gasped.

"That's not kind, Jonas Callahan!" She glared at him.

"It's true," Pete said. "Jackie gave me a bit of a rough road when she found out she was pregnant. There we were, this perfectly fine relationship—"

"That went on and on," Sam said. "Every woman has heard that a man who sleeps with her for a hundred years isn't serious about her, so you were only a Saturday-night fling, as far as she knew."

Pete stiffened. "But that wasn't how I felt about her. She just saw our relationship on a completely different level."

"I am never going through this," Judah said, "and if I do find a bride—and I hope I don't—but if I do, I'm going to do it right. None of this bride-on-the-run crap." He leaned back in the sofa, shaking his head.

"Maybe it's not that simple," Rafe said. "Maybe she didn't like it here."

"She didn't seem quite herself," Creed said, "but I

put it down to the fact that she was worried about her nieces." Yet he'd known deep inside that hadn't been all of it. "I guess she didn't love me," he said, not realizing that he'd spoken out loud.

"Did you tell her you did?" Rafe asked.

Creed glanced up from the letter. "Not specifically those very words. I mean, she knew I cared."

"Because she was clairvoyant," Sam said, nodding.

"Hey," Jonas said, "your time is coming, young grasshopper. Go easy on Creed."

"I'm just saying," Sam said, "that it's not like she's some kind of fortune-teller like Sabrina."

Everyone sent him a glare.

"Well, I did think she was the more quiet of the two sisters," Aunt Fiona said. "I wondered about it, I must say. I put it off to her being shy, perhaps, and—"

"That's why you offered Diane a job," Creed said, realization dawning like a thunderclap. He sent his aunt a piercing look. "You knew Aberdeen wasn't happy here, and you were trying to keep her little nieces here at the ranch!"

Fiona stared at him. "Oh, poppycock. That's a lot of busybodying, even for me, Creed. For heaven's sake."

He was suspicious. "Did Aberdeen tell you she wasn't happy here? With me?"

Fiona sighed. "She merely thanked me for my hospitality and said she had parents and a congregation to get back to. It wasn't my place to ask questions."

"So she never told you we'd had an agreement based on her feeling that a husband might put her in a more favorable light to an adoption committee?" Creed asked.

"So when Fiona offered Diane a job, and Aberdeen could see that things might be working out for her sister, the marriage contract between you two could be nulli- fied," Judah said, nodding wisely.

"Oops," Aunt Fiona said. "I had no idea, Creed. I was just thinking to help Diane get on her feet again."

It wasn't Fiona's fault. He and Aberdeen had an agree- ment which, to her mind, was no longer necessary, so she'd chosen to leave him. She couldn't be blamed for that, either, since he'd never told her that he was wolf- crazy about her. Creed grunted. "What happens if Diane doesn't accept your offer of employment?"

Fiona straightened. "She will." She looked uncertain for a moment. "She'd better!"

"Because you fell for the little girls?" Creed asked, knowing he had, too. It was going to drive him mad if they left—and yet, if Diane chose to leave with her daughters, he would wish them well and hide his ach- ing heart.

"No," Fiona said. "I would never dream of interfer- ing in someone's life to that extent. She just happens to have recipes from around the world, thank you very much, due to all her travels. And she has experience tak- ing care of elderly parents. And I could use a personal secretary." Fiona sniffed.

Groans went up from around the room. Fiona glared at her nephews. "Oh, all right. Is there anything wrong with giving a mother time to bond with her daughters? Perhaps all she had was a little bit of the blues. Does it matter? I like Diane. I like Johnny. And I like Aberdeen." She shook her head at Creed. "Of course I didn't mean to do anything that would give Aberdeen the license to leave you, but I didn't know the nature of your relation- ship. It was up to you to discuss your feelings with her, which I'm sure you did amply."

Creed grunted. "I was getting around to it."

A giant whoosh of air seemed to leave the room. His brothers stared at the ceiling, the floor, anywhere but at him. Creed's shoulders sagged for a moment. He hadn't, and now it was too late.

"Give her time," Fiona said. "If I was in her shoes, I'd want time."

He held on to this jewel of advice like a gold-miner. "You really think—"

"I don't *know*," Fiona said, "although all of you seem to think I know everything. I don't. I just think Aberdeen has a lot on her mind. I would let her figure it out on her own for a while, perhaps."

"It might be sound counsel, considering the lady in question is mature and independent-natured," Burke murmured in his soft Irish brogue. Burke didn't hand out advice willy-nilly, so he was sharing knowledge of how he'd won Fiona.

"And the baby?" Creed asked, his heart breaking.

Fiona shook her head, silent for once.

The minutes ticked by in still quiet. Creed read the letter again, feeling worse with every word. Judah got up, crossing to the window of the upstairs library. "The Diablos are running," Judah said, and though the joy of knowing the wild horses were still running wild and free on Callahan land sang in Creed's veins, he stared at out at them, not really believing their presence portended mystical blessings anymore.

Chapter Eighteen

Aunt Fiona's First Annual Rancho Diablo Charity Matchmaking Ball was a knock-out success, Creed acknowledged. Ladies of all makes and models came to the ranch by the carload. If he'd still been a single man, he might have been as holistically lighthearted as Sam, who was chasing ladies like a kid at a calf-catch. He thought Johnny Donovan garnered his fair share of attention, though the big man never seemed to do more than dance politely with any lady who lacked a partner. Jonas was his usual stuck-in-the-mud self. If anybody was ever betting on Jonas to finally have a wild night in his life, the bettor was going to lose his money to the house. Jonas was a geek, and that was all he was going to be.

The one shocker of the evening was that Judah and Darla Cameron—who'd had her eyes on Judah forever, not that his clown of a brother had the sense to realize it—actually seemed to engage in a longer-than-five-minute conversation. The chat lasted about twenty minutes, Creed estimated, even more surprised to see his brother initiate said conversation. To his great interest, he saw Darla head off, leaving Judah standing in the shadows of the house. Creed spied with enthusiasm, watching his boneheaded brother watching Darla walk away.

And then, just when he thought Judah was the dumbest man on the planet, beyond dumb and moving toward stupid-as-hell, Judah seemed to gather his wits and hurried after Darla. Creed snickered to himself and drank his beer. "Dumb, but not terminal," he muttered to himself, and thanked heaven he'd never been that slow where a good woman was concerned.

Or maybe he was. Creed thought about Aberdeen being up north, and him being here, and fought the temptation to give in and call her. Johnny said Aberdeen was stubborn. And on this Creed thought Johnny probably had a point.

He was willing to give her time, but it seemed like the cell phone in his pocket cruelly never rang with a call from her.

Creed went back to pondering Aunt Fiona's wonderful party. As bachelor busts went, it was one for the ages. Any of them should get caught. *Not me, I'm already caught, even if my woman doesn't know it. But it'll be fun for us all to get settled down, and then we'll raise a bunch of kids together, and instead of marriage feeling like a curse, we'll all look back and laugh about how determined we were to stay footloose and fancy-free.*

Except for my dumb twin. Rafe is a worm that will never turn. He watched Rafe go by, stuck in wolf mode, a bevy of absolutely gorgeous women tacked on to him like tails pinned on a donkey. Disgusting, Creed thought, that anyone considered his brother deep-thinking and existential when he was really a dope in wolf's clothing. Rafe looked like a man on his way to an orgy, dining at the table of sin with great gusto.

Disgusting.

Johnny sat down next to him on the porch swing. "You're not doing your part, dude. Aren't you supposed to be dancing?"

Creed shrugged. "I danced with a couple of wall-flowers, so Aunt Fiona wouldn't be embarrassed. But I'm wallflowered out now."

"Nice of some of the local guys to show up and help out with the chores of chivalry," Johnny said.

"Everyone loves a lady in a party dress," Creed said morosely. "Heard from your sister? She's not coming back tonight to make sure I have my dance card filled? Induce me to give up my swinging-single lifestyle?"

Johnny laughed, raised a beer to Creed. "You know Aberdeen. She's the kind of woman who'll let a man hang himself with his own rope."

Creed leaned back. "It's dangerous dating a woman who's fiercely independent."

Johnny nodded. "Tell me about it."

Creed gave him a jaundiced eye. "Oh, hell, no. You're not dating anyone. Don't give me that commiseration bit."

"I'm hanging on," Johnny said. "For the right one to come along and catch me."

"Yeah, well, good luck," Creed said. "I found the right one. She threw me back."

"Patience is a virtue," Johnny said, and Creed rolled his eyes. Patience was *killing* him. He'd never been a patient man. Fiona said that he'd always wanted every-thing he couldn't have. He was a worker, a planner, a man of action—the crusader who rode into a forest and plucked out a maiden in the midst of battle, if need be, even before he discovered treasure and liberated it from the evil dragon.

Princess first. Ladies first. Absolutely, always.

At least that's the way he'd always seen himself. Aberdeen had him sitting on the sidelines in his own fish story. He was chomping at the bit.

"Wanna dance, handsome?" Creed heard, and glanced up, fully prepared to wave off a charming and buxom beauty, only to realize she was staring at Johnny, her eyes fast to the man whom Creed had thought might be his brother-in-law one day.

"Mind if go do my duty?" Johnny asked Creed. "I hate to leave you here alone, nursing that dry bottle, but as you can see, duty calls, and it's a beautiful thing."

Creed waved the empty bottle at Johnny. "Never let grass grow under your feet."

"Nor your ass, my friend," Johnny said with a grin, and went off with a lovely lady dragging him under the strung lights and a full moon to join the other dancers.

Creed shifted, feeling as if grass might have grown under him, he'd sat here so long. Johnny was right: He was moping after Aberdeen. If he didn't quit, he was going to end up Rip Van Winkle-ish, waking up one day to find time had passed and nothing had happened in his life. The phone wasn't going to ring; Aberdeen wasn't going to call.

He was waiting on a dream.

He had a baby on the way, a child who would bear his name. But he couldn't force Aberdeen to love him.

He would just have to be happy with knowing that at least his future had a blessing promised to him. And he was going to be a hell of a father. Because he remembered how much it had hurt when he'd lost his own father, how much it had stung not to have a dad around on the big occasions. So maybe he couldn't be a husband, and maybe his Cinderella had thrown her slipper at his heart, but this one thing he knew: He was going to wear a World's Best Father T-shirt as if it was a king-size winning bull rider's buckle.

And his kid would know he was there for him. Always.

Eight months later

ABERDEEN HAD GROWN like a pumpkin: blue-ribbon, State-Fair size. At least that's the way she felt. Johnny worried about her incessantly. "You should have stayed, accepted the Callahans' offer of employment, because you're driving me nuts," she told her brother.

"I could have," Johnny said, turning on the Open sign at the bar door, "but my livelihood is here. I'll admit I toyed briefly with the idea of staying in New Mexico and working with the Callahans. They seemed to need the help. And they sure know how to throw a heck of a dance. There were ladies from everywhere just dying to find a husband. I had a feeling if I'd hung around, Fiona might have fixed me up with a wife, too. From what I've gleaned over the past several months, no weddings went off and no one got caught, though."

Aberdeen wondered if Johnny was trying to reassure her that no one had caught Creed. She decided to stay away from that painful subject. She nodded at his pleased grin. "You could use someone looking after you."

"Women are not that simple, as I know too well." Johnny smiled and wiped off the bar. "No, it was fun at the time, and I enjoyed the break, but I had to be near my new nephew."

She shook her head. "I don't know the sex of the baby. Quit angling for a hint."

Johnny laughed. "Okay. So what happens when the baby is born?"

"I'm going to keep doing what I'm doing. Occasionally preaching, working here, looking for a house."

Her answer was slightly evasive because she knew Johnny was asking about Creed. The truth was, she never stopped thinking about him. Yet she knew their bargain had been a fairy tale. He'd been grateful to her and Johnny; he'd wanted to help her out. She wouldn't have felt right keeping him tied to an agreement for which there was no longer a need.

"As soon as that baby is born, you know he's going to be here."

Aberdeen nodded. "That's fine." She was over her broken heart—mostly. "You know what the bonus is in all this? Diane is happy at the Callahan ranch. Her daughters are flourishing."

At that Johnny had to smile. He flew down there once a month to visit the girls and Diane, always bringing back reports of astonishing growth and learning skills. Teeth coming in. New steps taken. First pony rides. He'd even taken their parents down to visit once. They'd been impressed with the girls' new environment, and the change in Diane.

Johnny never mentioned Creed when he took his monthly sojourn to New Mexico, and Aberdeen never asked. She knew he would come to visit his baby. It would be the right thing, for the baby's sake. And he would want his baby to spend time at Rancho Diablo.

It will all work out, Aberdeen told herself. *We're two adults, and can make this work. We are not Diane and her ex-husbands, who turned out to be sloths and degenerates of the first order. Creed will be an excellent father.*

She turned her mind away from Creed and back to the new sermon she was writing. After the baby was born, she intended to go back to school for some additional theology classes. The bar would bring in some income as she did the books for Johnny, and then she could afford a separate house.

It might not be the kind of situation she'd dreamed of with her concussed cowboy—but those had been just dreams, and she knew the difference between dreams and real life.

She went upstairs to the temporary nursery, smiling at the few things she'd put in the small room. A white crib, with white sheets and a white comforter. A lacy white valance over the small window. Diapers, a rocker, some tiny baby clothes in neutral colors: yellow, white, aqua.

It had seemed better not to know if she was having a boy or a girl. She would love either.

In fact, she couldn't wait.

Voices carried up the stairs. Johnny was welcoming some customers. She'd be glad to find her own little house, she realized. Something about having a baby made her feel protective, made her need her own space.

Her tummy jumped with a spasm, bringing another smile to Aberdeen's face. This was an active child, always on the go. The ob/gyn had said that Aberdeen needed to take it easy; the baby could come any day now.

It was too hard to sit and wait, though. The feeling of

nesting and wanting everything just right had grown too great for her to ignore. She touched the baby's tiny pillow, soft satin, and told herself that in a few days, she'd be holding her own precious child.

"Aberdeen," a deep voice said, and she whirled around.

"Creed," she said, so astonished she couldn't say anything else. Her heart took off with a million tiny tremors. The baby jumped again, almost as if recognizing that its father had walked into the room.

"I bribed Johnny to let me up here without telling you I was here. Blame me for that, but I wanted to surprise you."

"I'll yell at him later," Aberdeen said.

His gaze fell to her stomach. Aberdeen put a hand over her stomach, almost embarrassed at her size.

"You look beautiful."

"Thank you." She didn't, and she knew it. Her dress was a loan from a mother in her congregation. She hadn't wanted to spend money on clothes when she was too big to fit into much other than a burlap potato sack, the kind that could hold a hundred pounds of potatoes easily. "Why are you here?" she asked, not meaning to sound rude, but so shocked by his sudden appearance that she couldn't make decent conversation.

She'd never been so happy to see anybody in her entire life. She wanted to throw herself into his arms and squeal for joy that he'd come.

But she couldn't.

"I came to see you. And my baby," he said. "I didn't want to miss you having the baby."

She swallowed. "Any day now. I guess Johnny told you."

Creed smiled. "He gives me the occasional update."

Drat her brother. "I guess I should have known he would."

"So this is the nursery?"

She ran a hand proudly along the crib rail. "For now. At least until I find a small house."

He nodded. He gazed at her for a long time. Then he said, "I've missed you."

She blinked, not expecting him to say anything like that. "I—"

He held up a hand. "It was just an observation. Not said to pen you into a corner."

She shook her head. "I know."

Another cramp hit her stomach. Her hands went reflexively to her tummy.

"Are you all right?" Creed asked, and she nodded.

"I think I'll go lie down. It's good to see you, Creed," she said. "Thanks for coming."

He nodded. "Guess I'll go bug Johnny. He's promised to teach me how to make an Expectant Father cocktail."

"Oh, boy," Aberdeen said, backing toward the door. "You two just party on."

She disappeared into the hallway, but as she left, she glanced over her shoulder at Creed. He was staring at her, his gaze never leaving her—and if she hadn't known better, she would have thought he looked worried.

If he was worried, it was because of the baby. He'd never said he loved her, never told her anything except that he'd take care of her and Diane's daughters, so she knew she'd done the right thing by letting him go.

Another cramp hit her, this one tightening her abdomen strangely, and Aberdeen went to check her overnight bag, just in case.

"So, DID THE heart grow fonder in absentia?" Johnny asked.

Creed shook his head and slid onto a bar stool across from Johnny. "Can never tell with Aberdeen. She keeps so much hidden."

"Have confidence," Johnny said, putting a glass in front of him, "and a New Papa cocktail."

"I thought you were going to teach me about Expectant Father cocktails."

Johnny grinned and poured some things into the glass. Creed had no idea what the man was putting in there, but he hoped it took the edge off his nerves. He'd waited eight long months to lay eyes on Aberdeen again, and the shock, well, the shock had darn near killed him.

He'd never stopped loving her. Not one tiny inch, not one fraction of an iota. If he'd thought he had any chance with her, any at all, he'd ask her to marry him tonight.

And this time he'd spend hours telling her how much he loved her, just the same way he'd spent hours making love to her. Only now, he'd do it with a megaphone over his heart.

"Give her a moment to think," Johnny said, "and drink this. It's for patience. You're going to need it."

"I've never had to chase a woman this hard," Creed grumbled. "I'm pretty sure even a shot from Cupid's quiver wouldn't have helped. The shame of it is, I know she likes me."

Johnny laughed. "No, this is a drink for patience as you wait to become a father. The doctor said today was her due date. Did I mention that?"

"No," Creed said, feeling his heart rate rise considerably. "All you said was today was a great day to get my ass up here. Thanks, you old dog. Now I think I'm going to have heart failure."

"You are a weak old thing, aren't you?" Johnny laughed again. "Relax, dude. I predict within the next week, you'll be holding your own bouncing bundle of joy."

Creed felt faint. He took a slug of the drink and winced. "That's horrible. What is it?"

"A little egg, a little Tabasco, a little bit of this and that. Protein, to keep your strength up."

Creed frowned. "Ugh. It's not going to keep my strength up, it's going to bring my lunch up."

"Trust me on this. It grows on you."

Creed shuddered. And then he froze as Aberdeen's voice carried down the stairs.

"Johnny?"

"Yeah?" her brother hollered up the stairs.

"I think perhaps you might bring the truck around."

Creed felt his jaw give. His gaze locked on Johnny. "What does that mean? Is that code for kick me out?"

"No." Johnny flipped the open sign to Closed and locked the door. "I think it means she wants to make a little run to the county hospital."

Creed blinked. He felt fainter. "What am I supposed to do?" He jumped up from the bar stool. "Should I carry something? Help her pack?"

Johnny said, "Hold on," and went upstairs.

A moment later, he came back down. "You might jog up there and keep an eye on her while I bring the truck around. I'll meet you out back in a minute."

Creed's anxiety hit high gear when he realized Johnny was totally rattled. The man knocked over a liquor bottle and broke a glass—Creed had never seen him anything but sure-handed around his bar—in his haste to put things away.

But he didn't hang around to analyze his friend. He shot up the stairs to check on Aberdeen. She sat on the bed, looking puzzled.

"Do you need something?" he asked. "A glass of water? A…hell, I don't know. What can I do?"

"Nothing," Aberdeen said, panting a little. "Except I have some concerns."

"Shoot," he said, "I'm your listening ear."

She gave him a wry gaze. "Are you going to want to be in the delivery room?"

"Nothing could keep me out of there," he said, "unless you don't want me, in which case I'm not above bribing you."

Aberdeen started to laugh, then quit abruptly. "Ugh. Don't make any jokes."

"I'm not joking in the least. I have to be there every step of the way."

"Okay." She took a deep breath. "You can't look under the sheet, and if things get tricky, you have to leave. Deal?"

"I don't know," he said, "you didn't keep to our last deal. I don't guess I can trust you with another one unless it's in writing."

"Creed!" Aberdeen said, looking like she was torn between laughing and crying.

"Oh, all right," he said, "although I reserve the right to judge what is tricky."

"If I say go, then you go," Aberdeen explained, with another gasp and a pant.

He sighed. "You'll want me there. Pete's already told me that my main role is to bring you ice chips and let you squeeze the skin off my fingers. Oh, and if you cuss me out, I'm to ignore all that and tell you how beautiful you are, and how you're the most wonderful woman in the world."

Aberdeen groaned. "If you can do all that, you'll be a true prince."

A truck horn honked outside, and Creed helped Aberdeen to her feet. "Guess I got here in the nick of time," he said, to make conversation. "Isn't that what princes do? Show up to help the fair damsel?"

Aberdeen didn't say anything for a moment.

But then she looked up at him, about halfway down the stairs. "Thank you for being here," she told him, and Creed's heart soared.

Maybe, just maybe…

Chapter Nineteen

"I can't believe my mother had six of us," Creed said, after Aberdeen let out a loud groan. "Can't she have some medication to dull the pain?"

"She's too far along," the nurse said.

"Can I have some pain medication?" Creed asked.

The nurse smiled at him, at the edge of tolerance. "Perhaps you'd like to go sit outside in the waiting area. We'll take good care of Mrs. Callahan."

Aberdeen let out another gasp. Creed's gaze flew to her, his teasing spirit gone. He was panicked. There seemed to be a lot of pain involved, and he hadn't meant to do this to her. She was never going to become Mrs. Callahan.

She was going to hate him forever.

He went through his litany of jobs Pete had suggested: Ice chips, tell her she's beautiful, stay out of the way except when she wants to squeeze your fingers to the bone. Try to be helpful. Try.

Creed stayed at the bedside, scared out of his wits. Good-and-stomped cowboys suffered, but even they hadn't seemed to be in this much agony.

Creed closed his eyes and prayed.

Thirty minutes later, Aberdeen gave one final shriek

that went through Creed—he seemed to feel her every pain—and suddenly the doctor smiled with satisfaction.

"It's a girl," the doctor said, and Creed went light-headed. He sank onto a chair as nurses scurried to clean up baby and Aberdeen. He was out of breath; there was no more strength in his body.

Then it hit him. The baby that was squalling up a storm and being fussed over by the nurses was *his*. He jumped to his feet and hurried over to get a glimpse.

She was beautiful.

He went to tell Aberdeen. His heart constricted as he saw how exhausted she was.

"How are you doing?" he asked, and Aberdeen gave him a wan smile.

"How are you?" she asked. "I thought you were going to fade on me."

"No," he said. "I'm tough. Not as tough as you, though. You win." He bent down and kissed her on the lips, so she'd know she was beautiful. A kiss seemed to express his feelings better at this moment than words.

Then he remembered he was in this predicament because he'd never said the words (Sam's shot about clairvoyance came to mind), so he just threw himself out on the ledge. "You're beautiful," he told her. "I may never get you pregnant again, but I want you to know that I love you fiercely, Aberdeen Donovan. And this may not be the time to tell you, but if you don't put my ring back on your finger and marry me, I'm going to…I'm going to cry like my daughter."

Aberdeen smiled. But she didn't say anything for a long moment. She closed her eyes and he thought she looked happy. Content. He brushed her hair back from her face, thinking she really was the most beautiful woman he'd ever seen in his life. Of course he was in love with her, had been always, but now she'd given him an amazing gift, so he loved her even more.

"I saw him one day," Aberdeen murmured, and Creed said, "Who?"

"The Native American. He was on your ranch, probably a thousand feet from the house. He waved to me, so I went to talk to him. He was tall, and had long, braided hair and such kind eyes. He said he was watching over the horses."

"The Diablos?"

"He called them that, but I didn't know what he meant at the time. And he said not to be scared, that all things worked out for the Callahans. That you would know your parents through this baby."

He blinked. "He told you that?"

"I didn't understand what it meant. But now I do. He said he'd known your parents a long time ago, and this baby was a gift to them. And then he left."

Creed was shocked. He'd never spoken to Aunt Fiona's friend; neither had any of his brothers, as far as he knew. "Our parents died long ago," he said. "I'm not sure how a baby can be a gift to them. But I'm okay with the theory."

"Have you ever talked to him?"

Creed shook his head. "He comes around to talk to Fiona about once a year. I don't know why. It's one of those things Aunt Fiona is mysterious about—one of many things, I suppose."

"He was nice. I liked him. I've never seen so much peace in someone's eyes." She looked at him. "I'll marry you, Creed Callahan."

His heart soared. "You will?"

She smiled. "Yes."

A nurse came between them for a moment, handing Aberdeen her pink-blanket-wrapped baby, and a delighted smile lit Aberdeen's face. "She looks just like you."

"Don't say that," Creed said, "I want her to look just like her wonderful mother. There are no beauties in my family tree, just unfortunately unhandsome brothers."

"There's a beauty now." Aberdeen kissed the top of her baby's head. "She's so sweet."

"That she gets from your side of the family." Creed was so proud he was about to burst. "Are you really going to marry me?"

Aberdeen handed him the baby, which he took carefully, lovingly. "I am, cowboy. I've decided you're the prince I've been waiting for."

He was so happy he wanted to cry. "What took you so long?"

"I was afraid you might be the wolf in my fairy tale, not a prince. You had me fooled for a while." Aberdeen smiled. "I was determined not to make any more mistakes. But I never stopped thinking about you, and after a while, I knew you were the only man I could ever love."

"When were you going to tell me?" Creed asked. "Because I'm pretty sure the last several months have just about killed me."

"After you told me," she said simply, and he groaned.

"I'm going to tell you every day of your life how much I love you," Creed said. "I'm going to keep you convinced that you made the right decision."

"I am," Aberdeen said with conviction. "I know exactly what I'm doing. I'm marrying the most wonderful man in the world. Now name your baby."

He hesitated, glancing down at the sleeping child in his arms. "I don't know anything about naming babies. What if I pick something she hates later on?"

She smiled. "Don't you have a favorite female name?"

"Aberdeen," he said with a decisive nod.

That made her laugh as she lay back against the pillow. "I'm going to sleep now, but when I wake up, I want you to have named your little girl. Surprise me with your creativity."

"No pressure or anything," he said, and he looked down at the tiny lips, adorable closed eyes, sweet cheeks of his daughter, knowing the old Navajo was right: This baby connected him to the past he could barely remember. But he knew his parents had loved him, just as he loved this child. Joy filled him, and then it came to him. "Joy," he said, and Aberdeen opened her eyes.

"That's lovely," she said.

"It's what I feel when I look at you," he said, and she knew his heart was in his words. "And when I hold this little baby…" He leaned down to give Aberdeen a kiss. "Thank you is all I can say. And I will love you until the end of time."

"You're going to make me cry," Aberdeen said, but he sat down next to her, and touched her face, and suddenly Aberdeen didn't feel like crying, only smiling, with joy.

Creed Callahan wasn't loco, she knew. He was her prince, her man, and the hottest cowboy she'd ever laid eyes on. All hers.

All her dreams come true.

Creed leaned against her and Aberdeen drifted, loving feeling him by her side, holding their baby. It was the sweetest moment, starting their family. She murmured,

"I love you," and Creed said, "Joy says you'd better," and then he kissed her again.

It was perfect.

Joy.

Epilogue

In February, the month after Joy Patrice was born, Aberdeen finally walked down the aisle into Creed's waiting arms.

Only it wasn't that simple.

First, he had to convince her that baby weight was no excuse not to marry him. Then he had to tell her that getting married at Rancho Diablo on Valentine's Day during the coldest month of the year was a swell idea—red was a great color for bridesmaid's gowns. She only had one attendant and that was Diane, but still, it took some doing. Aberdeen kept talking about waiting until springtime, when she'd lost some weight, when Joy would be a little older, when the weather would be warmer—but he wasn't about to let her weasel out of marrying him for any reason.

He'd nearly lost her before. If he'd learned anything, it was that he had to do a lot of talking with this woman. So talk he did.

And today, a day that dawned clear and sunny, he didn't relax until Aberdeen finally said, "I do." And even then, he asked her to say it again, which made her and the guests laugh.

Judah said later he'd never seen such a desperate case.

Jonas told Judah he'd better hush, because one day it might be him begging some poor woman to marry him. Sam said he thought it was romantic, if a bit weinie, of his brother to go down on bended knee and promise to love and adore Aberdeen for the rest of their lives, and Rafe said his twin had finally showed some depth of character and soul. Pete said he didn't care as long as they hurried up and cut the cake because he was starving. Keeping up with the demands of three little girls kept his appetite fired up.

Valentine's Day was a perfect day to catch his bride, in Creed's opinion. When they were finally declared husband and wife, he swept Aberdeen off her feet and carried her back down the aisle, intent on putting her right into the waiting limousine.

He intended to spend their week-long honeymoon in Bermuda making love to her constantly, and as far as he was concerned, the honeymoon began *now*.

"Wait," Aberdeen said, laughing, "Creed, put me down. We have guests. There's cake to cut."

"Oh." He put her down, reluctantly. "I'm not letting you out of my sight, though."

She took him over to the three-tiered cake. "I know. But there are some duties required—"

"Cut fast," he told her, and she made a face at him.

"We have to dance, and tell everybody thank you for coming," she said. "Creed, we just can't desert our guests. And there's Joy. I feel so guilty about leaving her. Don't you think we should wait for our honeymoon until—"

"That's it," he said, "here's the knife. Cut the cake, take a bite and let's shazaam before you get cold feet. I know you too well, parson, and I worked too hard to get you." He put cake into her mouth, waved at the applauding guests, let the photographer snap a few more photos of them, and then went over to Aunt Fiona who was holding Joy in her arms.

"This is a great party, Aunt," he said.

"But you're leaving."

He kissed her cheek. "Yes, we are. My bride wants me all to herself. Mrs. Callahan is demanding like that."

"Creed," Aberdeen said, laughing, as she bent to kiss Fiona's cheek, and then reached up to kiss Burke's.

"It's all right," Fiona said. "I've succeeded beyond my wildest dreams, so I just want to say welcome to the family, Aberdeen. And congratulations on catching Creed. I never thought I'd live to see the day, did you, Burke?"

Burke shook Creed's hand. "The limo has all your items in it, and is waiting for your call."

"Thanks for everything," Creed said, and kissed his aunt goodbye. Then he bent to kiss his baby's head. "Joy, you be sweet to your family. Aunt Diane is going to take very good care of you."

"Yes, I am." Diane closed her sister in her arms. "Congratulations, sis," she said, "I'm going to be as good an aunt to your daughter as you were to mine. I can never thank you enough for giving me time to figure out my life."

Aberdeen smiled. "I knew you would."

Johnny nodded. "I'm going to practice my uncle skills. I can't wait. Seems like I've been waiting months for this, and now I've got four babies to uncle. It's pretty cool."

"Yes," Creed said, prouder about new fatherhood than about winning all his bull rider buckles. "All these new women in my life. Who would have ever thought it?"

"I would," Fiona murmured to Burke, who hugged her as she gazed at her growing family. "I always knew he had it in him."

"I always knew I had it in me," Creed said to Aberdeen, and she kissed him.

"Let's go, cowboy," she said, for his ears only. "I've got a special gift to give you in the limo. Because I'm pretty sure you said I wasn't having you until I made an honest man of you, and now I have."

"Hot dang," Creed said. "I'm already there, my love."

They waved goodbye to their guests under a shower of pink paper hearts, and, as Creed helped his bride run to the white limo in her long, lacy gown, he caught sight of the black mustangs running, tossing their manes and pounding their hooves, free and wild, as they chased the spirits in the wind.

Enchanted.

* * * * *

Don't miss the next three
Harlequin Professional Bull Riders
collector's edition titles by Tina Leonard,
available now!

A FAMILY FOR THE BULL RIDER
HEART OF A BULL RIDER
THE BULL RIDER'S TWINS

MATT TRIPLETT

#3 MATT TRIPLETT
@triplett_matt

Matt started bull riding when he was ten, with help from his dad, who used to ride bulls, as well. He said although his grandfather was too tall to ride, he is still Matt's biggest fan. When he's not busy traveling the country entering in as many competitions as he can, he enjoys riding horses, hiking, feeding baby ducks at the park and playing basketball—his favorite team is the Indiana Pacers. He also loves watching football and cheers on the New England Patriots because of Tom Brady. His go-to meals are sushi, spaghetti and steak, but not all together, of course. Matt's most memorable ride was in 2013 in Grand Rapids, Michigan, on Pandemic (C'N Stars Bull Company) for 91 points during the Championship Round. During a bull riding in Montana, Pandemic kicked Matt in the stomach, causing him to have internal bruising, so he says it was his way of getting back at the bull. He also added that the injuries didn't stop him from riding. He loved riding in Anaheim because of how close it is to Disneyland. He visited the amusment park last year and plans to go again each year the PBR visits. You can find the twenty-three-year-old hanging out with Ryan Dirteater, Douglas Duncan, Chase Outlaw, Sean Willingham and Gage Gay on tour. He also works out with Douglas year-round doing hot yoga and visiting Michael Johnson Performance.

Meet Professional Bull Rider
Matt Triplett!

So, Matt, how did you get into bull riding?

I grew up on a little ranch in Columbia Falls, Montana, and I grew up watching my dad ride bulls, and he's been my hero all my life. So what better way than to follow in his footsteps? That's exactly what I did, and he taught me everything I know and showed me the ropes of bull riding—and that's how it got started.

What's been your most memorable ride so far?

I think it's yet to come. I still have a bright future ahead of me, and so I'm just ready for it.

What's your idea of a romantic evening?

My idea of a romantic evening—well, it would start with a couple's massage, then I would take her to the fanciest restaurant in town and then end by having a glass of wine and sitting in a hot tub.

HARLEQUIN®

American Romance®

ROMANCE THE ALL-AMERICAN WAY!

Save $1.00

on the purchase of
THE COWBOY'S HOMECOMING
by Donna Alward, available
May 5, 2015, or on any other
Harlequin® American Romance® book.

Coupon redeemable at participating
Walmart outlets in the U.S.A. only.

Save $1.00

on the purchase of any Harlequin® American Romance® book.

Coupon valid until August 5, 2015.
Redeemable at participating Walmart outlets in the U.S.A. only.
Limit one coupon per customer.

5 65373 00076 2   (8100)0 12030

PROFESSIONAL BULL RIDERS

SAVE 25%
ON SELECT TICKETS*
USE CODE:
BOOK15

PBR BUILT FORD TOUGH SERIES

THE PROFESSIONAL BULL RIDERS

The Professional Bull Riders (PBR) was created in 1992 when a group of 20 bull riders broke away from the Professional Rodeo Cowboys Association and started an exclusive circuit for bull riders. In little more than two decades, the dream of 20 bull riders has become a global sports phenomenon, reaching more than half a billion households in 50 nations and territories worldwide.

Declared America's fastest growing sport by Forbes.com in 2013, the PBR boasts a fan base of over 24 million. More than 2.5 million fans attend live events each year.

More than 600 bull riders from the USA, Canada, Brazil, Mexico and Australia hold PBR memberships and compete in more than 300 PBR owned and sanctioned bull riding competitions domestically and internationally, all trying to qualify for the elite Built Ford Tough Series (BFTS), which will feature 27 stops in 18 states in 2015. The season will conclude at the Built Ford Tough World Finals in Las Vegas on October 21–25, where the PBR World Champion will be crowned and receive the coveted championship buckle, valued at more than $10,000, and a $1 million bonus.

The Built Ford Tough Series is televised every week on CBS, CBS Sports Network and networks around the world. For more information on the PBR, go to PBR.com, or follow on Facebook at facebook.com/PBR, Twitter at twitter.com/PBR and YouTube at youtube.com/PBR.